ENTICED BY A SAVAGE

MONI LOVE

FOLLOW ME ON SOCIAL MEDIA

Facebook Like Page: Moni Love

Instagram: Author_moni.love

Twitter: Moniloveland

OTHER BOOKS BY MONI LOVE

Is Love Enough Part 1&2 (completed series)

Once Upon A Hood Love: A Compton Fairytale

Finding Love At Christmas With A Cali Boss

Enticed By A Savage

PARIS

Summer 2013

O*hhhh oh ohhh*
     All I see is signs
All I see is dollar signs
Ohhhh oh ohhhh
Money on my mind
Money, money on my mind

It was the Fourth of July weekend, on one of the hottest days of the summer. My best friend Dream and I were out cruising the streets of Los Angeles in my brand new 745i Mercedes Benz, listening to Rihanna's new song, "Pour It Up." We were looking for something to get into as we cruised through the city with the top down and our hair blowing in the wind. Since we were on the west side, I decided to pop up on my boyfriend, Quincy. I knew more than likely he was hanging out in his hood, shooting dice doing dope boy shit, so I took the short drive across town to see what he was up to. I knew he would be upset because he and my father hated me being in the west side area of Los Angeles. There was always ongoing beef with them east side niggas.

Fifteen minutes later, we pull up on 112th Street and Raymond

Avenue— the block was hot. All the neighborhood dope boys, hoodrats, and hustlers were hanging out smoking weed and listening to trap music loud as fuck. I spotted Quincy right away standing in front of the big house, which was the spot. He was squatted down shooting dice with a wad of cash in his hand, looking fresh as always.

"Paris, is that Q right there?" Dream asked, pointing in his direction.

"Girl, yes, that's my baby. I'm about to get out and go say what's up to him." I smiled licking my lips, while double-parking my car in the middle of the street. "I see Chris over there with him, are you getting out the car, friend?"

"Hell no, fuck Chris. He plays way too many games for me. I'm not thinking about his lying ass!"

"Ok well, I'll be right back. Roll up the weed, Dream."

"Alright boo, I got you."

I opened the door to my ride, and before I could even step out the car, all eyes were on me as usual. Today I was dressed for the beach since the weather was hot. I was rocking blue denim booty shorts and a red bikini top with red Chanel sandals on my feet.

Crossing the street, I walked up behind Quincy with a smile on my face. I couldn't even control how happy I was to see my man.

"Q!" I called out to him. He turned towards me with a mug on his face.

"Paris, why you standing behind me while I got the dice in my hand? You know I hate that shit!"

"Really, Q?" I snapped, ready to go off on him.

"Yes, really!" he mocked me standing to his feet, walking over to me. "Baby, what the fuck I tell you about coming to the hood? You know it's not safe for you over here. Niggas can pull up and wet this block up at any time!"

"I know, babe, but I missed you. I texted you earlier, and you didn't respond," I whined.

"That don't mean pull up in the hood because I take too long to reply to your text, ma. You know how it is when I'm on the block. I'm in the middle of a dice game, that's why I didn't answer. It's bad luck."

"You so full of shit, bae." I laughed, wrapping my arms around his neck. "You over here with Chris' hoe ass. Let me find out you got some bitch stashed away, Quincy!"

"Man, knock it off. You're my only bitch." He chuckled, kissing my lips.

"Don't play with me, Quincy!"

"You know I always reply to your text eventually. I know you don't really have a fuckin' attitude, right? He asked while grabbing a handful of my ass. I smiled, eating up the attention that I was receiving from him.

"Nah, boo, we're good."

"Give your nigga a kiss. Make that shit nasty too." I happily slid my tongue in his mouth, not giving a damn about the entire block watching us.

"Damn, Q! How the fuck you gone interrupt the dice game to go cupcake with Paris' big lip ass?" His homie Larry snapped in irritation. Before I could react, Q checked him.

"Nigga, watch yo fuckin' mouth when you address my woman before I murk yo ass!"

"Tell him, baby!" I teased, giving Larry the middle finger. "Don't get yo ass beat on this beautiful summer day!" I snapped at Larry hating ass.

He always had something negative to say every time I saw him. He stayed taking shots at my lips. However, I could care less about what a hater had to say about Paris Monroe. I don't like the disrespect. I've always been secure about myself and always confident in the way I looked.

Standing at five foot seven, with caramel colored skin, beautiful bright brown eyes, full lips, and long hair, I knew I was the shit. My slim thick frame, along with my dope personality, is the reason a lot of these niggas and bitches in the city hated on me for no reason. Niggas hated because they wanted what they could never have, and bitches hated because that's what lame bitches do.

"Paris, get off the block and go home. I'll be there around seven to pick you up."

"Where are we going?"

"Let's go to the movies tonight."

"Alright babe, I'll go home. My dad just got back in town, so I'll just hang with him until you come pick me up."

"Alright that's cool, Tell Don-Don I said I need to holla at him in the morning."

"I will, but you already know he's gone be bitching about you sending messages through me instead of calling yourself."

"Man, yo pops been on some other shit lately, so I don't even want to deal with him half of the time."

"I think he's just going through something. It's probably something about business, but I will talk to him and see if I can figure out what it is."

"You don't have to do all that, it's cool."

"Are you sure?"

"Yeah, I'm sure. Is that Dream in the car with you?"

"Yeah that's her. She didn't get out the car because she didn't want to see Chris."

"Man, tell her to stop acting funny with the homie. She knows damn well she loves his ass."

"That may be true, but Chris needs to learn to keep his dick in his pants." I smiled, shaking my head. "Let me get out of here because I have to take Dream home. Please don't be late, Q."

"I'm always on time, baby. I'll see you later." He laughed. "Now get yo sexy ass off the block and go home and wait on your nigga to get there. Make sure you wear something sexy for me tonight too."

"I got you, bae. I already have the perfect outfit in mind." I smiled, kissing his soft lips twice before I walked away.

⚶

An hour later, I pulled up to the Monroe Estates, my beautiful eight-bedroom, contemporary style, childhood home. I was so happy to see my father's Rolls Royce Phantom parked in the driveway. He's been in and out of town for the last two weeks distributing coke from state to state. I hated him being gone so much, but I knew it was a part of the game, and he had to provide for our family, so I never nagged him.

"Daddy!" I entered the house and ran to him as I've always done since I was a little girl. I hugged him tight like I hadn't seen him in years.

"What's going on firstborn, how is my princess?" He embraced me, kissing my forehead.

"I'm eighteen now, dad. Shouldn't I be the queen?" I laughed, kissing his cheek before pulling back.

"That would be a negative. Your fine ass mama is the queen around this castle," he teased.

"You and your sister are my two princesses. Oh yeah, before I forget, what's this I'm hearing about you being on the west side today? I thought I told you to stay from over there, Paris Monroe!"

"I'm sorry, dad. I was only over there for maybe fifteen minutes. I only stopped by to say hi to Quincy."

"I see." He walked away with a displeased look on his face.

"Why did you just walk away, dad?" I whined, following behind him into the kitchen. He poured himself a glass of Hennessy, giving me a strange look that I couldn't read. "What is it, dad?"

"I love you daughter, but Quincy is not the nigga for you."

"What? I thought you liked Quincy. Where is all this coming from?"

"I love Quincy like a son, but you're my daughter. You were supposed to be the heiress to my empire when I retire, but you chose to do things your way. I've allowed you to choose your own path in life. However, I will not allow you to ruin your future dealing with Q. You need a man who will be able to provide you with a better life than I have provided for you."

"I can't believe you're saying this, dad!"

"It's the truth, Paris. I hope this is just a little phase you're going through. You need to date someone who brings out the best in you. Do you think I don't hear how you and Dream be in the streets chasing behind Q and Lil Chris knucklehead ass! I've taught you to never chase behind any man. Don't ever forget your worth firstborn," my father scolded me like a small child. "Your mother was never like that with me. She's never had to chase me. If anything, she protected me and my vision. When necessary, she stepped up to the plate and was right beside me riding shotgun. How do you think I've been so successful over the years, Paris?"

"Wait, dad, I've known Quincy for years now, and we've been together for a minute. This isn't just a phase. I love him. We are not you and mom, and we're not striving to be. Y'all have written your story already. Please allow us a chance to do the same. You can't tell me how to live my life and who to be in a relationship with. This is not the 50s. I know Quincy is far from perfect, but he's perfect for me. He loves and respects me for who I am, not because of the Monroe legacy that's attached to my name. Besides you never hear his name in the streets, like you hear Chris', so please don't put him in the same category as Chris' dog ass."

"Watch your tone, Paris Monroe."

"I apologize, but you have to excuse me. I just don't know where this is coming from. However, I need you to understand I'm not breaking up with Quincy anytime soon. What we have is real. Now, if you would excuse me, I have to get ready for my movie date in a few hours."

"I love you, princess. I only want what's best for you, that's all. Go ahead to your room and get ready for your date." He kissed my cheek then walked out of the room, shaking his head.

Later That Night

What was supposed to be a simple date to the movies, ended up being a wild night at the strip club. I was only eighteen, so tonight was my first time going to a strip club, and it definitely won't be my last. The vibe inside the club tonight was off the chain. It was nothing like I expected. I spent my night chilling with Quincy, his homies, and their beautiful women. Club Oasis had nothing but the best of the best working in their establishment. The assortment of exotic beauties dancing on stage left me in a trance for most of the night. The way some of them chicks could make their booty pop, and ass shake, put my twerking to shame. We partied hard all night, leaving the club right before closing. I must have blown through a few stacks of bills before the night ended. Now my man and I were riding through the city late night/early morning— vibin', listening to music, enjoying each other's company.

"I'm hungry as fuck, Paris."

"Shit me too, bae. Let's go to Denny's in Hawthorne," I suggested, staring at his handsome face.

"Shit, I'm wit it, a nigga bout to get his grub on. It's been a long ass night."

"It has been a long night. You said we were going to the movies, but you took me to Club Oasis instead, so that's your fault." I shrugged, turning to look out the window.

"Didn't you have fun?"

"I have fun wherever I go. You already know that I'm the life of the party, Quincy." I smiled, enjoying the night air blowing on my face.

"I think you enjoyed the strippers more than I did." He laughed, placing his right hand

on my exposed thigh.

"I had a good time tonight, babe. I can't even lie. Dream and I will definitely be back next month for her eighteenth birthday. We about to turn the club all the way up!" I laughed, dancing around in my seat, mimicking the moves I saw the strippers doing tonight.

As we pulled up at the light on Crenshaw and King Boulevard, I stopped acting silly to check my appearance in the mirror. I had to make sure my lip gloss was still popping. Quincy's right hand began working its way up my thigh, moving between my legs.

"You always starting shit, bae," I voiced as he pulled my panties to the side.

"I can't help it. Look at yo sexy ass sitting over there," he uttered, pushing his middle finger inside of me. I released a low moan while closing my eyes, throwing my head back. "Damn Paris, that pussy stays wet for a nigga," he expressed, kissing my lips hungrily while stroking my insides.

"Q, baby, that feels so good," I moaned, feeling my orgasm approaching.

"Fuck! Paris, baby, we gone have to finish this when we get back to my crib. The light about to turn green," Quincy groaned, removing his hand from my wetness.

"Fuck that light, babe," I huffed, opening my eyes watching him lick my juices off his fingers. Before I could say another word, the sound of glass shattering caught my attention. I sat up quickly with wide eyes, now on alert.

"Paris, you strapped? My pistol is still in the trunk from earlier!"

In a state of panic, I reached down on the floor, feeling around for my Chanel bag. Inside was my 9mm that my father made me carry around at all times for my protection. Somehow, the strap to my purse was hooked on something underneath the seat.

"I can't get it, Q! It's stuck on something underneath the seat!" I panicked while trying to get it loose.

"Fuck! Just keep trying!" A tall, heavyset masked man unlocked the driver's side door through the broken window, then snatched it open.

I began to panic, trying to figure out my next move. Now in survival mode, I quickly surveyed my surroundings. It was at that moment I realized we were both fucked. Quincy's truck was surrounded from all angles. The masked man snatched Quincy out of the car by his shirt, throwing him to the ground with a loud thud. He was talking shit, making the situation worse. Q was wasting his breath because there was nothing he could do to help us out of this situation. Moments later, my door was snatched open, and I was looking at a Glock .45 in my face.

"Don't say a fuckin' word bitch, or I'll blow yo fuckin' brains out!" the second masked man yelled, pressing his gun in my face.

"You must not know who the fuck my father is! If you did, you wouldn't have that gun in my face! If it's his truck that y'all want, just take it and go. Just please leave us alone!" I pleaded not wanting them to take either one of our lives. The masked man looked me in the eyes and began laughing.

Confused by his response, he then went on to say, "Little mama, if you only knew who sent us." He continued to laugh, gripping the handle on his pistol tight, refusing to back down.

"Paris, fuck these niggas! If they gone kill me, then so be it. I love you, ma!" Quincy expressed, bringing tears to my eyes.

"Q!" I called out to him.

Seconds later, my heart dropped as I began screaming at the top of my lungs. The sound of gunfire erupted, so I dropped down to the floor of the car.

"AHHHHHHHHH! AHHHHHHHHHH! OH MY GOD, PLEASE! SOMEBODY HELP US!" I screamed in horror, shielding my eyes from broken glass and shell casings flying everywhere.

Tattttttttttttttt tattttttttttttttt ttattttttttttt! Tatttttttttttttttttt tattttttttttt taaattttt! The sound of powerful semi-automatic weapons had my ears ringing, and my heart beating at a rapid pace.

When the shooting stopped, I took that brief moment to reach down underneath the seat to free my purse. As soon as I had it in my trembling hands, I searched inside for my pistol. I quickly checked to make sure the safety was off, then hopped out the truck, firing my weapon until the clip was empty. The second masked man dove for cover into the driver's seat of the getaway car, skirting off in the distance. I damn near burned myself putting my smoking gun back in my purse, then ran to Quincy as fast as I could.

I let out a gut-wrenching scream from the depths of my soul when I saw him shaking and convulsing on the ground. Quincy, my first love, and closest friend, was left to die in a puddle of his own blood. His entire body was riddled with bullets right in the middle of Crenshaw Boulevard. I didn't even think twice when I fell to the ground getting blood all over my clothes. After seeing his condition, I cried uncontrollably while cradling Quincy's near lifeless body in my arms as he struggled to breathe. I'll never forget the scared look in his light brown eyes as he stared directly into my mine, gasping for air. I could tell he was trying to talk, as blood poured out both sides of his mouth like a faucet.

"Shhh, don't talk. Save your energy," I mumbled in a low tone. "Baby, I love you so much," I cried, feeling helpless. "Please help us!" I continued to cry while rocking him back and forth in my arms. "Q, hold on baby. Help is on the way." I wanted to put on a brave face for him, but the tears just kept falling.

"I lo-love you too," he finally uttered, coughing up blood. Seconds later, his eyes started rolling in the back of his head as his body convulsed.

"Please hold on Quincy. I can hear the sirens from the ambulance. They're getting close, Q."

Minutes felt like hours had passed before the paramedics finally arrived on the scene. After checking Quincy's pulse, he was immediately pronounced dead. In that instance, my heart stopped beating momentarily. Hearing those words ripped my heart into pieces.

"Noooo! Noooooooooo! Quincy, baby, get up! Please don't leave me like this. You said you loved me. Remember you promised me forever!" I cried, standing over his lifeless body.

"Sweetie, please calm down. I'm sorry for your loss, but please allow us to do our job, young lady." One of the female paramedics grabbed me, pulling me away from Quincy's body.

"Get your hands off me! Don't you touch him! Maybe if it wouldn't have taken y'all twenty minutes to get here, he would still be alive!" I snapped, putting up a fight. A male police officer approached me instantly pissing me off.

"Please back up, Miss. This area is now being treated as a crime scene. Please come with me so that you can answer a few questions about what went down here tonight!" the officer spat in a rude tone.

"Get your fat ass away from me. I'm not telling you shit! If you want to talk, I'll give you the number to my family lawyer!"

"Just calm down, young lady."

I tried my best not to flip out, but once I saw them covering Quincy's body with a white sheet, I lost it.

"Stop it, nooooooooo! Please leave him aloneeeeee!" I screamed, swinging at everyone in my sight.

I didn't want to be bothered. I was angry, hurt, heartbroken, and inconsolable. Suddenly my head started spinning, and I felt lightheaded. The last thing I remembered was collapsing on the ground staring up into the moonlit sky, feeling a sense of calmness come over me as my world faded to darkness.

§

I woke up hours later to my parents, my sister Lundyn, and my father's henchmen surrounding me in my hospital room. Me being a daddy's girl, I jumped right into his arms while he held me like a baby. I cried so hard that my hands were trembling and my teeth were chattering. My father allowed me to cry until I didn't have any tears left. It felt like a piece of my soul had been snatched from me without warning. I've known Quincy since elementary school. He was not only my first love, but he was my friend before anything. He was my first kiss, and the first and only person I had been intimate with. I loved him with everything in me. Now my heart felt shattered, my soul crushed.

There was no coming back from this type of pain. Quincy and I had that young hood love that people envied. I thought we would be together forever. I didn't know how I would go on with my life without him. How do you wake up one day, after spending every day with someone and expect to move on with your life when they are no longer there? That question was continually running through my mind. That means I have to figure out a way to go on with my life without waking up to a good morning text, or late-night phone calls. All I'm left with is this feeling of emptiness in the pit of my stomach. I literally felt numb.

About an hour later, I was able to calm down and get control of my emotions long enough for the doctor to release me to my father. The police showed up right when we were leaving to question me, but my dad wasn't going for it. He gave the detectives the number to our family lawyer and then sent them on their way. Afterwards we left Centinela Hospital in Inglewood and headed to our house in Gardena.

"Princess, are you awake?" My dad asked, rubbing my head while I laid in his lap.

"Yes, dad, I'm up."

"I know this is hard on you right now, but I promise things will get better. Just take everything one day at a time, love."

"I will, daddy. It just hurts so bad." I wiped my face as the tears began to fall again.

"You know it wouldn't be me if I didn't keep it real with you. Q was a street nigga, and this so happens to be one of the consequences of being a street nigga. Although it may hurt losing him, try to focus on the fact that he loved you wholeheartedly. He was one of my best workers. Quincy was like the son I never had. It was a blessing for him to be a part of your world, firstborn."

"I loved him, dad. He was my world." I continued to cry.

"You will always be my princess, and you will always have me, Paris. Even though you didn't want to take your proper place as heiress of the throne when I retire, I still love you more than you will ever know. You're my firstborn."

"I love you too, dad. Can we please talk about something else? Anything but Quincy, not right now, dad. It's too soon. This wound is still fresh."

"You got it, princess. When we get home, I'll have Maria make your favorite banana pancakes. What do you say?" my dad suggested, leaning down to kiss my cheek.

"No, it's too early, dad. Besides, I'm just not in the mood to eat."

"I understand. Come on. Sit up. We're home now." I sat up, stretching my arms over my head. My dad's driver Derrick came around to open the back door for us. I stepped out of the car first with my father right behind me.

"I hope Lundyn is sleep because I don't feel like answering a bunch of questions from her. It's six in the morning."

"We made it home before the sun came up, so I'm sure she's sleeping. I sent her and your mother home a few hours ago."

"I kind of figured that much, dad." Walking up the cobblestone walkway to the front door chills went down my spine. As I surveyed my surroundings, I knew something was off.

"Dad, something's not right. I have a bad feeling."

"Princess, come on, you've had a long night. You need to get some res—"

My dad barely got the words out of his mouth before federal agents swarmed the front yard. FBI and DEA both swooped in tackling my father to the ground. I stood there with my eyes bucked wide open, realizing what was happening. Moments later, the front door was kicked in, and the Feds raided the house. After destroying our beautiful family home, my mother was dragged out of the house, in handcuffs, while wearing nothing but a tank top and a lace thong. The agents read her, her rights then placed her in the back of the FBI van, separated from my father.

My little sister and I stood around and watched in disbelief as all our possessions were tagged then confiscated by the Feds. All my clothes, shoes and even my brand new car was taken from me. By the time the Feds finished, we were left with nothing. All I had were the clothes on my back, whatever was in my purse and my cell phone. I knew that after tonight my life would never be the same. *Shit just got real!*

Chapter One

PARIS

Six Years Later

I f six years ago you would have told me that I Paris Monroe, daughter of the infamous Adonis 'Don- Don' Monroe would have been through everything I endured these last few years, then I would have probably laughed in your face. I grew up a spoiled princess, a daddy's girl who had the world laid at my feet. My father, Adonis Don-Don Monroe, being one of the biggest drug distributors of the '90s and mid-2000's spared no expense when it came to his family. There was no way I would have thought my world would all come crashing down in the blink of an eye, but it did.

Today was probably one of the happiest nights of my life. Some may laugh at me because I'm glad about finally closing this chapter of my life, but I thank God I didn't get sucked into the dark side of making fast money. I've seen a lot of shit working in this industry, so that's why I promised myself to focus on the main goal, which was stacking my paper, making sure my family was taken care of. I promised myself to finish up school, which I did a little over a year ago, then get out as soon as all my goals were met.

From where I stood behind the stage, I could feel the vibrations from the club's speakers underneath my feet. The potent smell of the best Cali weed lingering in the air, mixed with the fluorescent lights flashing throughout the club had my adrenaline pumping. When the DJ cued my performance song of the night "Dirty" by R&B singer Tank, all the nervousness I felt instantly disappeared. I was more than ready to hit the stage for one last time. This was my final set, and I've never been more excited about anything since the day I watched my little sister graduate from high school a couple of years ago. For the last five years, I've been shaking my ass in Club Oasis, running up a check securing the bag a couple of nights per week. I was one of the most highly requested strippers in the city. What most people didn't know about me was that I was 'Desire' when I walked through the door of this club. However, that wasn't my day to day life. Yeah, I shook my ass some nights, but by the morning, I was Paris Monroe the pretty chick with a regular life working a 9 to 5.

"Coming to the stage for the last time. I want everybody in the muthafuckin' building to give it up for the beautiful, sexy, the one and only Desireeeeeeeeee!" DJ Poo shouted me out, and the club went crazy.

Fuckin' you deep, takin' pics on my phone
Yea, dirty.
Put you to sleep when you wake up, its dawn...

I adjusted my signature masquerade mask that somewhat hid my identity before I hit the stage wearing a black lace Fendi thong bodysuit with five-inch stiletto boots on my feet. I was in a trance-like state working the crowd moving my body seductively to the beat. The lustful stares from the men and women watching me dance gave me all the motivation I needed to keep going. I looked out into the crowd to find the nigga in the room whose demeanor screamed boss nigga. I spotted who I was searching for in seconds while he stood in the cut, watching me intensely. He was tall, brown skinned, very handsome with a muscular build. I could tell by the way he carried himself he was the savage type who ran shit. He was so fine, and the way he kept eye fuckin' me while he blew smoke rings in the air had me feeling some type of way.

When our eyes connected, I used my finger to call him over to me.

As he made his way over to the stage, I dropped it low, popping my pussy a few times while grinding my hips. He had the sexiest grin on his face as he made it rain using crisp one-hundred-dollar bills. The feel and smell of the money being rained down on me had my body tingling all over. Every time I heard the sound of another band pop, my pussy got wetter and wetter. This is definitely something I was going to miss about hitting the stage. Some women like shoes, or designer bags, some even preferred diamonds, but as for me, money made me cum.

Chapter Two

JINX

Little mama who hit the stage last was bad as fuck— no cap! I came out tonight strictly on some business type shit, but when Desire came out and hit the stage, she had a nigga stuck like she put a spell on me. I'm Jinx Kingston, leader of the Savage Boyz and all around boss ass nigga. I've never been the type of nigga to be impressed by a stripper hoe, but she had a nigga mesmerized and my dick so hard that it hurt. When she waved me over to come closer to the front of the stage, I was gone turn around and walk away, but after seeing her climb up that pole and pop her ass cheeks while working her way down into a full split, my legs moved before my mind could say no. She was a sexy ass redbone with a pretty smile and deep set of dimples. The mask she wore on her face barely concealed her identity. She was average height, curvy in all the right places, with thick thighs, and a nice ass that was fat and juicy.

When I got to the front of the stage, she squatted down in front of me seductively rubbing her breasts, while biting down on her bottom lip. When she took her hand and lightly tapped that fatty between her thighs, I had to make it rain on her one time to show my approval of her performance. We were in a packed strip club, but I swear to God, in that moment, it felt like it was just the two of us in the room. I had dropped about ten stacks on her pretty ass by the end of her set, and it was worth every dollar.

"Damn nigga, you was feeling that bitch, wasn't you?" my bro Gunna laughed when I walked back into VIP.

"No cap, that bitch was bad, nigga!"

"For the right price she will probably let you fuck." He laughed, drinking straight from a bottle of champagne.

"I'm good. I'm not even on that shit tonight."

"If you say so." He shrugged. "Had that been me, I would be in the backroom knee deep in some pussy."

"Well, luckily, you and me are not the same muthafucka." I laughed, popping a bottle of Ace.

"How much longer do we have to wait on that nigga Dray to get here?"

"He should be here any minute, now chill out G. The last thing I need is for you to be on that bullshit."

"Jinx don't be tryna check me like I'm some hoe ass nigga. It's two things I don't like wasting, that's my time and my money. If there ain't a problem with the two of them, then we good."

"Here that nigga come right now."

"Who is these clown ass niggas Dray got with him?"

"How the fuck am I supposed to know? They won't be around while I'm conducting business I know that much."

"Facts bro."

"Sup Jinx? Gunna?" Dray spoke before giving us pound.

"Same shit different day. Aye, who are these niggas you got with you?"

"These are my homies, Mook and Drew. I know you don't mind them being here, do you?"

"Actually, I do mind!" I snapped, rubbing my hand through my beard. "Can you send them away while we're trying to conduct business, nigga?"

"Come on, Jinx. These are my people, they straight."

"Aye, check it out, Dray. I don't know either one of these muthafuckas. Either you can send them to get a dance from one of these strippers, or you can get the fuck on with them."

"It's cool. I understand." Dray turned to his homies sending them away. "Alright now, where were we?"

"Let's be clear, the next time you have to meet with me concerning business, come by yourself. Don't ever show up with a bunch of weird ass niggas I don't know thinking you finna get put on cause it ain't happening. Is that understood?"

"With all due respect, Jinx. You are not about to be talking to me like I'm some soft ass nigga. Business is business, and I'm tryna break bread with you, so if my money ain't good with you no matter who I'm with, then I can take my money and go elsewhere, my nigga."

I laughed, firing up the blunt behind my ear and waited on what I knew was coming next. *5,4,3,2,1!*

"I tried bro, but you know I'm the rebellious type."

Bam! Bam! Bam! Bam! Gunna hopped up, jumping over the table, going across Dray's shit with his pistol, leaving his face leaking.

"Now, not only are you not doing business with the Savage Boyz, but you also finna walk out of here with one hunnid stack less then you came in with, pussy," Gunna hissed, snatching Dray's duffle bag he walked in with that was filled with cash. "Yo, Jinx, where did you find this goofy ass nigga at?"

"Ugggghhnn!" Dray groaned, rolling around on the ground, holding his nose.

"Nah, nigga, don't cry now. I bet the next time you won't walk up to a business meeting late on some rah-rah shit!" Gunna laughed, placing his pistol behind his back.

"I call myself doing a solid for Tino. Wait till I see his tall, skinny ass tomorrow, bro. Somebody come get this nigga the fuck up out my section!" I roared.

Minutes later the club bouncers came and dragged Dray out of VIP like the piece of shit he was. He should have known better than coming at a savage like me any ole kinda way. I don't deal with fuck shit, and he was no exception. Gunna was twenty-one and very much a hot head. He didn't give a fuck about anything, but stacking his bread, guns, the gang, and his brothers. Me being his big brother, he protected me at all cost, and that was vice versa.

I finished my blunt then picked up my bottle of Ace, taking it straight to the head. That's when I noticed Desire making her way across the room. She must have gone to freshen up because she wasn't wearing the same thing from when she was on stage earlier. Now she wore red booty shorts with a black sparkly bikini top with some heels at least five inches high. No lie little mama was looking good enough to eat. The way her fat pussy ate up the shorts she was wearing had my dick brick again.

"Here comes ole girl from earlier. You need to be tryna see what that mouth do, nigga. I'll be back in a minute." Gunna laughed before walking away.

"What's up daddy, you want a dance?"

"I think this one should be on the house," I smirked, roaming my eyes all over her thick frame. I zeroed in on her pretty feet and couldn't help licking my lips.

"Guess what boo, tonight is your lucky night. You were a big money spender this evening, so I owe you this dance."

"That's what the fuck I'm talking about, ma." I smiled, rubbing my hands together like Birdman.

"Come on, daddy. Let's go upstairs. Since this is my last night at Oasis, I might as well give one last private dance in the VIP room."

I didn't even object when Desire grabbed my hand leading me out of my section to the VIP room. The security standing outside the room let us in when we reached the door. "Have a seat love while I go put on something sexy to dance to."

"What's your name, lil mama?" I asked, taking a seat on the plush couch in the corner of the room.

"Desire," she replied, looking over her shoulder.

"Nah, ma, what's your real name?"

"I try not to mix my business life with my personal life, but I'll make the exception for you this once." She smiled, revealing her deep dimples.

"Why are you wearing that mask when you're not on stage? You do know it's not hiding very much, right?"

"I have a life outside of this place. I wear this mask because I don't want to let what I had to do to survive ruin what I've worked so hard for these last few years," she voiced, removing the mask.

"Damn ma, you bad as fuck. No cap!

"Thanks," she called out over her shoulder. "My name is Paris, by the way. What's your name?"

"It's Jinx."

"I just told you my name, but you gave me your street name. Why is that?" She turned to look me in my eyes with a displeased look on her face.

"No bullshit, Paris, Jinx Kingston is my real name?"

"You are telling me your mama named you Jinx?" she asked face twisted up in confusion.

"The shit's fucked up, right?" I laughed, rubbing my hand through my thick beard. "My mama was a dope fiend; what you expect?" I chuckled, shrugging my shoulders.

"I apologize. I promise I wasn't trying to be rude. I thought you were being funny."

"It's cool. Most people think Jinx isn't my name, and I'm fine with that. Do you mind if I smoke?"

"It's cool, do your thing. All I ask is that you give me your undivided attention."

"Aye, real shit Paris, you've had that all night! Make sure I get my money's worth," I smirked, licking my lips.

Chapter Three

PARIS

"I always aim to please daddy," I flirted, while seductively biting down on my bottom lip. As the music started to play, I popped myself on the ass making my booty jiggle like a tidal wave. The lustful look in Jinx's eyes had goosebumps all over me.

"Do your thing, lil mama," he grinned, nodding his head up and down giving me his approval.

"I like it when you lose it
I like it when you go there
I like the way you use it
I like that you don't play fair."

The sultry sounds of Tank's hit song "When We" played over the loud-speakers. I dropped down into a squatting position while swaying my hips from side to side. Popping back up, slithering my body like a snake, I slowly grind my hips in a circular motion to the beat.

"Who came to make sweet love? Not me
Who came to kiss and hug? Not me
Who came to beat it up? Rocky
And don't use those hands to put up that gate and stop me."

. . .

Seductively dropping to the floor, I got down on my hands and knees, crawling over to where Jinx sat on the couch smoking a fat ass blunt. Once I made it directly in front of him, I straddled his lap then began grinding my hips giving him a ride he'll never forget. When I felt his erection growing underneath me, my eyes bucked feeling how big he was.

"Don't get scared now. Let me get my money's worth, ma," he smirked, taking another pull of the potent weed that he was smoking. Sliding off him back down to the floor, I laid on my back pushing my legs behind my head. Jinx had the perfect view of the fatty between my thick thighs, so I took my hand and patted my pussy, before using my middle finger to circle my clit over the thin fabric of the shorts I wore. Feeding off his energy, I slowly slid my middle and index fingers in my mouth. As he took two deep pulls from his blunt, he reached down into his other pocket, pulling out a stack of bills.

"You must be tryna take all my money tonight, Paris." He chuckled, taking another puff from his blunt. When I began moaning while sucking my fingers, making slurping sound, he sat up watching me like a hawk while making it rain on me once again. "Got damn ma, you sexy as a muthafucka," he mumbled, before sitting back adjusting his hard-on. I was stuck in a trance-like state watching him, thinking nasty thoughts.

The eruption I felt brewing deep within me caught me off guard. I didn't know what it was about Jinx, but his presence was stirring things up inside of me that I haven't felt in years. Focusing back on the task at hand, I found my way to his lap again, working my hips like a skilled belly dancer. It made no sense how wet I was. The friction from me rubbing against him was creating a mess in my now soaked shorts.

Smack!

"Ahhh sshit, Jinx!" My body trembled under his touch as I rocked back and forth against his erection, imagining he was deep inside of me. Every nerve ending in my body was on fire as he held a firm grip on my backside. "Sssshit," I moaned, tossing my head back enjoying the tingly sensation flowing through my body.

"You about to cum, ain't you?" he uttered while nibbling on my neck.

As the next verse of the song started, I slowly slid off his lap, down to the floor, teasing him by sitting my pussy right in his face.

I could be aggressive (I could be aggressive)
I can be a savage (I can be a savage)
I just need your blessin' (I just need your blessin')
Say that I can have it, yeah
When we fuck,
When we fuck

My mind was so far gone that I didn't even realize I had zoned out until I felt Jinx pull the center of my shorts to the side, exposing my goodies.

"Damn yo shit is dripping like water," he mumbled, using his thumb to circle my clit.

"Ummm ahhhhhh yesss!" I cried out as he continued circling my clit at a rapid pace. "Yessssss, oh my god, I'm about to cum, Jinx! Please don't stop!"

"Let that shit go, Paris," he groaned, adding his middle finger inside of me, while his thumb worked my clit driving me insane. "Ummm hmm, there you go witcho sexy ass!"

I lost total control of my senses at this point. My body began to tremble after cumming back to back. I collapsed to the floor with my eyes closed, trying to gain control of my senses.

"You good?" Jinx laughed, pulling me up onto his lap, wrapping his arms around my waist. It took me a minute before I finally came back to reality, but when I did, shame immediately took over me.

"Yes, Jinx, I'm fine. I am so sorry! You probably won't believe this, but I have never done anything like this before."

"No need to apologize, ma. I can tell you needed to bust that nut." He laughed, gripping my ass with both of his hands.

"Give me one second. I'll be right back." I ran off to the bathroom to freshen up, feeling ashamed of my actions. About ten minutes later,

I emerged from the bathroom surprised to see Jinx still sitting on the couch waiting for me.

"You sure you alright?"

"Yes, I'm fine. I'm surprised to see you still sitting here tho." I smiled nervously.

"I'm waiting for the rest of my dance. You zoned out halfway through the first time."

"That was so embarrassing." I smiled, taking a seat next to him on the couch.

"Can I ask you a question?"

"Umm.... yeah sure why not."

"What are you doing working in a place like this? I can tell you're different from the rest of the chicks that dance here."

"I never in a million years thought I would ever strip, but then life happened and things changed."

"How long have you been dancing?"

"I started working here a few years back looking for a quick way to make money."

"You could have done anything. There are many different ways to make fast money, so why this?"

"My only other option was selling coke, and I had no interest in being a dope girl. I always knew that I could dance, so that's what I chose to do. I remember my first time going to the strip club, right after I turned eighteen. I saw how much money some of those girls made in little to no time. So when I found myself in a bind, that's what I chose to do. I did give the whole working in fast food thing a try, but it just wasn't for me either.

"Where are your folks at? You couldn't go to them for help?"

"I can't believe I'm telling you my personal business in the VIP room." I gave an awkward laugh.

"I just wanna know your story, but If you're uncomfortable, you don't have to tell me."

"It's cool Jinx, but let me make this very long story, short for you. When I was eighteen all in a days' time, I witnessed someone I loved dearly get murdered right before my eyes."

"I'm sorry to hear that Paris, it's a cold world so unfortunately, shit like that happens every day."

"It's been a while now, so it doesn't hurt as bad. Anyway, my dad came to pick me up from the hospital the same night I witnessed the murder. When we made it back to the house before we could even get inside, the Feds swarmed us then raided my childhood home arresting both of my parents."

"Damn, are you serious, Paris?"

"As a heart attack. It was one of the craziest times of my life. I was constantly going back and forth to court. My life was just crazy back then."

"I bet it was, ma."

"While all that was going on, I still had a fifteen-year-old sister who needed me. I was of legal age, so luckily the state didn't remove her from my care, but at the end of the day, shit got real overnight."

"Are your folks still locked up?"

"Yeah, my dad beat most of his charges, but the judge gave him and my mother both ten years for conspiracy and money laundering. The coldest part is that they only gave my mother time because she wouldn't fold on my dad.

"That's fucked up lil mama, but that's all a part of the game."

"I know that now, but at eighteen, it was a lot to deal with all at once."

"I respect you for stepping up to the plate to look after your sister."

"She's my heart, Lundyn is twenty-one now, so she's pretty much on her own."

"I salute you Paris real shit."

"Thanks. I'm just glad I'm finally able to move on from this chapter of my life and focus on my career now."

"You did mention tonight was your last night, so I thought you meant that you were changing clubs." He laughed.

"Nah I'm giving up on making fast money. I've basically been living a double life."

"Why is that?"

"I'm a college graduate, Jinx. If I told you what I did for a living, you would probably side eye me."

"Oh ok I get it now. That's why you be wearing the mask when you dance."

"Bingo!" I smiled playfully hitting his arm. "Usually, I dance three to four nights a week. Then by morning, I'm dressed in my business attire headed to work. It gets exhausting."

"Why didn't you quit when you started working?"

"I wanted to save some money up, so that's what I've been doing for the last year. I make a lot of money dancing, but it's time for me to move on."

"What do you plan on doing with the money you saved?"

"You ask a lot of questions." I smiled, leaning into him."

"I'm interested in what you have to say, shit I can't help it." He laughed, placing his hand on my thigh.

"I want to open up some type of boys and girls or nonprofit organization for troubled kids. I love kids, and somehow, I want to make an impact on the world starting with our youth because they are the future."

"Damn Paris, not only are you bad as fuck, but you're smart too. That shit is rare and sexy."

"Thank you. You're really trying to gas my head up I see." I smiled, laying my head on his shoulder.

"I don't think I've ever met a chick quite like you before, no cap."

"You probably never will, Jinx. I wasn't always this way, but life has a funny way of humbling you." Smiling, I stood up on my feet. "Are you ready to head out? I think I'm ready to call it a night."

"Yeah, we can roll out. I'm about to get up out of here too after I find my brother. Let me get your number, Paris. Maybe we can link up in a few days."

"If we ever cross paths again, then I promise I'll give you my number. I've already told you my life story, so if it's meant to be, we will meet again."

"Are you serious right now?"

"Dead ass serious, Jinx. I really enjoyed talking to you tonight. My last night at Oasis has been very interesting."

"Alright bet. I know we will cross paths again sooner rather than later."

"I look forward to it, boo," I smiled walking out of the VIP room.

I planned to give a few lap dances, but I was honestly over the club scene. I lingered around for another thirty minutes having a drink, watching one of the only girls I was cool with finish her set before I went in the locker room to change again. Afterwards, I got my bag out of my locker then checked my appearance in the mirror. I was wearing distressed black leggings, with a baby tee and Fendi sneakers. I gathered my money bag stuffing it inside of my backpack then left the locker room, waiting for security to walk me out to my car.

A Few Hours Later

At 6:55 in the morning like clockwork, I woke up trembling in fear during the same part of the dream I kept having. Quincy was trying to tell me something, but his voice would always fade away before I could hear what he was saying to me.

Getting out of bed, I went to handle my morning hygiene. I smiled at my reflection in the bathroom mirror, happy that I didn't look like what I had been battling mentally over the years. After brushing my teeth, washing my face, and moisturizing my skin, I went to get dressed for work. Today will be busy for me since I'm working in the field for most of the day. I decided on wearing a black pants suit with a pair of nude peep-toe red bottom stilettos. Just recently, I was promoted to the lead position in my unit at Child Protective Services, so I liked to dress the part. I grabbed my tote with my iPad and caseload files for the day, picked up my keys, and headed downstairs.

"Good morning, sis!" I greeted my sister Lundyn, who was sitting on the couch, watching reality TV as usual.

"Top of the morning, Paris! You headed to work?" She smiled, looking up at me.

"Yeah, I'm in the field today, so I have to get an early start. What you got going on today?"

"I have a client this morning, and then I'm going out to lunch with Rasheed."

"I'm so proud of you. You're really doing your thing down at the shop."

"Thanks that means a lot, Paris." She smiled, standing up to walk me to the door.

"Don't forget about Dream's party tomorrow."

"How could I? You two bitches have been bugging me about it for the last two weeks."

"Because P, you be tripping sis. You don't like to go out and ever have fun. Everything is always about work with you."

"I gotta make sure the family is straight. Therefore, I only have time to mind the business that pays me boo. I know I danced, but I hate the club scene if that makes sense."

"Yeah ok Paris, the party is Friday, and that's tomorrow, so get it together, love."

"I'll be there, but only because I would never let my bestie down. Have a good day, Lundyn."

"Later, boo."

When I stepped outside the sun was shining brightly in my eyes. Pressing the button on my key fob, my G-Wagon unlocked then started right up. After placing my tote in the trunk, I grabbed the file for the first location I was headed to and put it on the passenger seat.

While I drove through Gardena headed to the east side of Los Angeles, my stomach began to rumble. I made the mistake of forgetting to eat breakfast once again this morning, so I would have to stop and grab something before my first home visit.

Fifteen minutes later, I was around the corner from my destination on 93rd and Main Street. I pulled up to the SB Market that was on the corner of Main Street and parked right in front of the door. After locking my car up, I walked inside to see if I could find me a muffin or donuts to put on my stomach.

Ding Dong!

The alarm beeped when I walked in the door, startling me. I was taken back by how nice and clean the store was. I could tell it had been recently remodeled. From the outside, it appeared to be just another hole in the wall mom and pop store. However, the inside was the total opposite.

"Sup, ma?" The store clerk bobbed his head at me, walking from the back of the store.

"Hey, good morning." I smiled, not even bothering to look up as I walked around the store looking for something to snack on.

"You need some help?" The store clerk asked, walking up behind me.

"Actually, you can help me. Where are the donuts or muffins at? Do y'all have any? I can't find them anywhere.

"Yeah, they're up towards the front, ma." The way he said *ma* immediately made me teary-eyed, reminiscing about my first love Quincy. "Aye, are you alright? Why do you look like you're about to cry?"

"I'm so sorry. You just reminded me of someone that's all." I smiled, wiping at the tears in my eyes. When I turned around looking up into his eyes, I froze. "Jinx?"

"The one and only." He smiled, revealing his perfect white teeth. "You sure you good, ma? I don't know what I did, but I wasn't tryna make you cry."

"Yes, I promise I'm fine. I just had a moment it happens from time to time." Walking towards the front of the store, I found the items I was looking for then placed them on the counter.

"Yooooo Tino! Come up front, we got a customer. Ring her up so that I can get out of here. I got moves to make, nigga!" he yelled to someone in the back.

"Can't you ring me up?"

"Yes, I can ring you up, but that's what I pay my employees for," he smirked, licking his juicy lips. *Damn, he's handsome.*

"Oh, this is your store? My bad I thought you worked here?" I inquired, being nosey.

"Yeah, this is my shit, Paris. I own a few businesses on this block. If I'm not mistaken, I dropped way over ten stacks on you last night in the club, and I couldn't get that type of money working at a place like this."

"I don't know why I didn't think about that before."

"It's cool. You don't see a lot of young black men who own businesses."

"I love to see black-owned businesses. I'll definitely try to support your other ones."

"You blow trees?"

"You mean like smoke weed?"

"Yes."

"Nah, I haven't smoked in years. why do you ask?"

"If you don't blow, it's not important. Let Tino ring you up so that you can get out of here."

"I'm actually only headed right down the block to my client's house, so I'm in no hurry."

"Client's house?"

"Yeah, I'm a social worker."

"Wait, how does that fit into your night job?"

"It doesn't, so that's why I quit."

"So you were serious?"

"Yes, Jinx!"

"Oh ok, that's what's up. It all makes sense now. Do you remember what you said to me last night before we went our separate ways?"

"We talked about a lot of things last night. Refresh my memory."

"You said if it were meant to be, then we would cross paths again and here we are." He laughed while rubbing his hands together.

"What are the odds we would cross paths this soon?"

"Sounds like it's meant to be." He shrugged with the sexiest grin on his face I've ever seen.

"I guess that means you're taking me to dinner. I don't want no cheap date either so put some thought into it." I smiled, taking my iPhone out of my purse. I unlocked my phone then passed it to him.

"Lock your number in then call my phone so that I can have your number."

"I got you, Paris.

Ring! Ring!

"I got it boo. I'm gonna lock your number in."

"Aight cool. I'ma call your fine ass in a few days, so make sure you answer my call."

"We shall see. Well let me pay for my things so that I can get to my client's house."

"Don't worry about it, I'll see you around, Paris."

"Later, Jinx." I waved before walking outside to my car. After eating my blueberry muffin and washing it down with orange juice, I headed to my client's house around the corner.

Knock, Knock!

"Ms. Moore, are you home?"

Knock, Knock!

"There's no one home, sweetheart. I saw the oldest boy leave with the younger siblings this morning for school, and he hasn't been back since," the middle age woman who lived next door informed me from her doorstep.

"Thank you, ma'am. Do you mind letting them know that Ms. Monroe stopped by? Here is my business card." I smiled politely handing her the card.

"I sure will hunny." She smiled, taking the card from me.

After getting back in my car, I pulled off headed to my next client's house. I could already tell today was going to be a long day.

Chapter Four

LUNDYN

"Come on, Paris, it's just one night. It's wrong for you to leave Dream hanging on her birthday. She's your best friend!"

"Dream knows exactly how I rock. That's my bestie. I'm sorry Lun, but I don't want to go out anymore. She will just have to understand."

"She won't. She told me earlier she really wanted you to go."

"I can't, Lundyn. My caseload was full today, and I'm super tired."

"It's just one night, sis. Stop using your job as an excuse for everything."

"It's the truth. With my new promotion comes a lot more responsibilities. I have a home visit first thing in the morning."

"On a Saturday?"

"Yes. I have to do a pop-up since my client has been avoiding me all week."

"I promise we don't even have to stay long."

"Lundyn, I just can't do the club scene tonight. I'm over it. I danced in a club for years, so I'm in no hurry to go back. Besides, I know there will be some type of drama. There always is."

"Nothing is going to happen tonight, I promise."

"You don't know that for sure, Lundyn.

"Yes, I do! Now let's find you something to wear. We're going to Club Reign tonight."

"No, I'm not!" I turned, walking off.

"You're definitely going. It's about to be a lituation tonight boo." I laughed, following Paris out of the family room.

꙳

It was after ten p.m. when I finished getting dressed. I was excited about going to Club Reign tonight since It was Freaky Friday. The dress code was grown and sexy, so I had my sexiest shit on. Dream had rented out the entire main section in VIP for her birthday, so it was definitely about to be a movie. Although Dream was Paris' best friend, we had a great relationship and partied hard together. Paris was always too busy to go out and enjoy life like a normal person her age. Dream was bougie as hell, but she knew how to turn up and have a good time, so we clicked.

While sitting at my vanity staring at my reflection in the mirror, I had to admit I was one bad bitch. I beat my face to perfection, adding my signature glossy lips for that extra pop. Every time I did my makeup, I got better and better at it. Hair and makeup had always been something I enjoyed doing. It was kind of like therapy for me. It wasn't until maybe a year and a half ago that I started taking it seriously and making money from it. I created a business page on Instagram showcasing my work, which helped tremendously with building up my fan base. Soon after, I quickly put my plans in motion to become a full-time licensed professional hair and makeup artist. During the process, I ended up dropping out of school at Cal State Long Beach to enroll in beauty school. I initially hid what I had done from Paris thinking that she would be disappointed in me. It turns out she was proud that I made the decision to follow my dreams.

Fast forward to now, I have my own suite at one of the most popular salons, Ty's Beauty Bar, in Compton. It felt good to know that I had my sister's full support. With my parents both being in prison, I needed her support more than anything.

After checking my appearance in the mirror once more, I dabbed my favorite Chanel perfume behind my ear, then picked up my clutch, and iPhone before walking out of my bedroom. I went to the kitchen to make me a drink while I waited for Paris to finish getting dressed.

"Girl, I know you fucking lying! Lundyn, where is the rest of your clothes?" Paris asked with a shocked expression on her face as she walked into the kitchen.

"It's right here." I laughed, spinning around.

I had on this cute black lace two-piece short set that Fashion Nova knocked off from Kim Kardashian. I knew how to look good on a budget, so there was no shame in my game. Standing at five-feet-six and one hundred fifty pounds with a naturally curvy body, my caramel colored skin tone, complimented my light brown oval-shaped eyes. I had deep dimples that I inherited from my mother and long hair. I kept it bone straight most of the time. I knew I was gorgeous, and you couldn't convince me otherwise.

"Lundyn, you are doing the most with this outfit. This is why I don't party with your young ass. I thought I was the stripper, not you?" Paris nagged me as usual.

"You mean ex-stripper," I smirked, being sarcastic.

"Don't make me drag your ass."

"I'm just messing with you. Lighten up, sis. It's just jokes. Seriously Paris, I'm twenty-one now, so that makes me grown, boo. You are only twenty-five, and you need to start acting like it."

"Lundyn, I know how old I am. I know I work your nerves, but it's only because I've been looking out for you for so long. I'm proud of the beautiful person you've blossomed into, but I can't lie to you. I miss my baby sister," she whined, taking a seat.

"I'm right here boo. I appreciate you more than you will ever know, P. You have done more than enough for our family without ever complaining."

"Thanks that means so much to me, Lundyn."

"Enough of this sensitive shit, let me make us a drink so that we can go. You're driving tonight."

"See, Lundyn, I knew you were going to pull that shit. Let's go before I change my mind!"

"I'm coming, wait in the car while I finish making this drink." After

I finished mixing my drink, I set the house alarm then walked out to the car.

"It took you long enough!" Paris complained.

"Stop complaining and drive, Paris! Oh yeah, I forgot to tell you Dream needs you to come pick her up too."

"What? I promise I'm never going anywhere with you again."

"I love you too, sis." I laughed, pissing Paris off even further.

Chapter Five

PARIS

"Damn, I knew we should have come earlier. It doesn't look like there is anywhere to park," I sighed, pulling into the parking lot of Club Reign, the most exclusive nightclub in downtown Los Angeles. After circling the lot twice, I drove right up front into valet parking. The line to get inside the club was so long that it was damn near wrapped around the corner. Luckily, for us, Dream was VIP status and had an entire section reserved for her guests. That meant there would be no waiting in long lines for us. Everyone standing in front of the club was staring at us hard trying to see who was about to get out of my new ride. The sounds of Cardi B's song "Press" could be heard outside from the loudspeakers blasting in the club. After checking my hair and makeup in the mirror, I blew myself a kiss satisfied with my look.

"Let's do this. Are y'all ready to get out?"

"You already know I am, Paris. I'm so glad you came out tonight," Lundyn voiced from the passenger seat.

"Me too, I hope I don't run into anybody from the strip club. I hate that shit."

"Paris, just relax, and please don't be tripping on me once we get inside. I need you to remember you're my sister, not my mother."

"Girl, just don't embarrass me or do no stupid shit, and we're good Lundyn."

Opening my car door, I stepped out of my G- wagon wearing a black mini dress with some badass Fendi heels on my feet. Dream and Lundyn were dressed like some freak hoes, but they still looked good. I did a double take once I realized we had the attention of everyone standing in line to get in the club.

"Aye, what's up cutie? Let me get yo number," some guy standing in line called out to me.

I ignored him and kept walking over to the valet worker handing him my car keys. He, in return, gave me the ticket that I would need to get my car back whenever I was ready to leave. As we walked the short path to the front entrance, a group of guys was headed there at the same time we were. Thinking they would let us go inside first because we were ladies, I got a rude awakening. As I made it halfway to the door, the guy leading the pack bumped into me. The impact was so powerful that I went crashing to the ground landing right on my ass.

"Damn excuse you, asshole!" I screamed feeling embarrassed. I was literally in shock while Lundyn helped me off the ground.

"I swear you L.A. niggas don't have no respect nowadays!" my best friend Dream spat, but my ass was embarrassed. The nosey onlookers standing in line were pointing and laughing at me, which really pissed me off.

"I know you saw us walking, fuck boy! You could have waited until after we got inside before you went in with yo rude ass!" Lundyn snapped, facing the guy who knocked me down. Dream's bougie ass stood there looking prissy but ready for whatever as always.

"Who the fuck you do think you talking to?" the rude asshole hissed getting in Lundyn's face.

"Gunna?" She stepped backwards looking like she had just seen a ghost.

"Damn, ma, it's been a minute," the guy Lundyn referred to as Gunna changed his angered facial expression to a huge grin almost immediately.

"You know this fool, Lundyn?" I asked, confused by their sudden awkward interaction. She turned to me with a look of disappointment after mushing him in his face.

"Nah, I don't know this nigga. Let's go inside, P." She smacked her lips, still backing away from him.

"Oh, you don't know a nigga no more, Lundyn?" he snapped, getting in her face. I just knew he was about to hit her, but he did the total opposite. He leaned down passionately kissing her lips while she stood there like a fool moaning and enjoying the moment with her eyes closed.

"You out here cappin' for these bitches you with, when you know exactly who the fuck I am. Don't worry. I'm not gone fuck you up for mushing me only because I know you probably still mad at a nigga. You got that Lun, enjoy your moment." He looked over to me. "Next time step aside when you see the Savage Boyz walking through," he smirked before walking inside of the club.

Lundyn stood completely still, not saying a word.

"Umm, that was awkward. Who the hell is that, Lundyn?"

"That was Gunna, an old friend from high school." She sighed, looking like she wanted to break down and cry.

"Are you ok, sis? He must be important if he has you on the verge of tears."

"Let's just go enjoy the rest of our night. I don't want to talk about him right now."

"Ok, but just tell me who was all them niggas he was with?"

"I don't know any of them but Gunna. They were probably his homies from his crew the S Boyz."

"The S Boyz? Girl good night, I cannot!" I laughed, leading the way inside the packed club.

"Paris, my section is upstairs. Come on, let's go this way," Dream pointed as she led the way upstairs. When we made it to the top, the VIP suite to the left of us was full of niggas.

"Oh Lord, what are the odds our section would be right next to the S Boyz," Lundyn rolled her eyes, flopping down on the couch.

"What does the S stand for?"

"Savage."

"Oh, I should have known." I laughed to myself. "I don't know what happened between you and Gunna, but don't let it ruin your night, sis. You got me out of this house, so we are going to enjoy our night. Fuck him."

"Ok that part, bestie! It's my birthday, so I need y'all to get it together. I'm about to get us some bottles so that y'all can loosen up."

"You're so right Dream, happy birthday once again friend. Please don't turn down for Lundyn or me. Tonight is all about you, and I'm here to celebrate with you."

As I was talking two bottle girls walked up the stairs carrying bottles of liquor, juice, ice and Red Bull energy drinks, placing everything on the table.

"Excuse me, but I didn't order any of this stuff," Dream explained in confusion.

"This is from the S Boyz." The bottle girls smiled before walking back downstairs. We all looked at each other smiling from ear to ear.

"Let's just enjoy the free liquor and not think anything else of it."

"Make me a drink, bestie. Let's crack that Hennessey open."

Dream picked up three cups filling them with ice. I poured me a glass of Hennessey by itself with just a little ice. I did the same for Dream and Lundyn only I added Red Bull to theirs before handing it to them.

"Yasssssss, Paris! I needed this drink. It's my birthday come on y'all let's turn up.

Chapter Six

JINX

I couldn't keep my eyes off Paris as I sat in my section in VIP smoking on some fire ass weed. I was beginning to think this was the universe way of telling me she was supposed to be a part of my world. This will be my third time in two days running into her fine ass. I sent bottles over to her to see how she would act once she got full off that liquor. The night I met her at the strip club, she seemed like a real cool chick that was just doing what she had to do to get ahead in life. However, at the same time, I also come from the streets, so I know things are not always as they seem. When people drink, they usually reveal their true self. I planned to sit back and observe her until she noticed me. Hopefully, the person I briefly got to know in the VIP room is who she really is because that person was dope as fuck.

As I watched her from where I sat in VIP, I couldn't help but wonder why her sexy ass was sitting by herself while her friends were up dancing having a good time. She must have felt me staring at her because she turned to look in my direction, and our eyes connected. Since I had her attention, I waved her over to me. I could see her eyes roll upward, but eventually, she got up and walked over to me.

Damn, she is bad as fuck, I thought, rubbing my beard, which was something I did when I was in deep thought or irritated. Her body was sculpted like a work of art. The tiny black dress she was wearing hugged her curves just right. Her wide hips swayed seductively from side to side with each step that she took demanding the attention of everyone in the room. Paris had nice melon size breasts that were on full display. Directing my full attention down to her thick thighs, I wanted to pick her pretty ass up and wrap them muthafuckas around my neck while I taught her all about that savage life. Like a creep, I kept roaming my eyes all over her body searching for at least one flaw but found none. Damn, she even got pretty toes. My dick bricked up instantly looking down at her freshly manicured toes. I had to adjust my shit in a hurry before she noticed the large bulge in my jeans. I had a slight foot fetish, and Paris had nice feet so I couldn't help myself from lusting over her.

"Hey, what's up, boo?" She smiled nervously pulling her long hair behind her ear.

"You nervous, ma?"

"No, not at all. I can't believe we keep running into each other like this." She smiled. Her smile was so bright, and not one tooth was crooked or out of place. *Damn, she's perfect.*

"Yeah, that's the same thing I thought when I saw you sitting across from me. What are you sipping on?"

"Hennessy, I actually need a refill."

"Here drink some of this champagne." Popping the cork on a bottle of Ace of Spades, I poured some out then filled her glass to the rim. She took a sip of her champagne looking at me lustfully. "So, is Jinx really your name?"

"Didn't I tell you it was the first time you asked?"

"Yeah, but were you serious."

"You nosey as hell woman!" I laughed. "To answer your question though, yes, my name is really Jinx."

"That's interesting you look more like a Tyrin or Jayceon. I just would have never guessed Jinx." She laughed.

"Oh, I see you got jokes." I smiled standing up from the couch walking up on her. "Anybody ever tell you that you have some big ass lips?"

"Jinx, please don't talk about my lips."

"I never said something was wrong with them. I like them. They're big as fuck tho," I teased.

"Whatever I hear this all the time about my lips, but I'm used to it, so it's cool." She laughed playfully hitting my arm.

Lifting her chin, I stared down into her big oval-shaped eyes. It felt like a jolt of electricity shot through my body, so I did the first thing that came to mind. I leaned down kissing her on her lips that were pillow soft.

"Ummmmm!" she moaned, pulling back from me.

"My bad Paris, I couldn't help myself. This ain't even how I rock normally, but I want yo sexy ass in the worst way."

"It must be destiny." She laughed to herself. "Let's just chill tonight. I'm usually a good judge of character, and I'm feeling your energy, Jinx. Otherwise, I would have slapped you when you kissed me."

"My bad, Paris. I couldn't help myself. Who is that you came here with tonight?"

"Oh, that's my sister I was telling you about Lundyn and my bestie Dream. It's her birthday tonight.

"Oh ok, that's what's up. It's my bro's birthday tonight too. The gang and I are out tonight celebrating."

"Wait, are you from S Boyz?"

"What you know about the gang, Paris?"

"I don't know anything. I'm asking because I ran into one rude ass nigga tonight, and my sister said he was from S Boyz."

"Aye, calm down killa I didn't do it." He put his hands up in surrender.

"You're right, my bad. He was just such an asshole."

"I started the Savage Boyz when I was a young little nigga on the come up. Every nigga from the gang is solid as fuck, so just let it go ma."

"I'm over it."

"You got an attitude now?"

"Nah, my feet hurt. I need to sit down," she admitted. "These heels are for sitting being cute, not standing, walking, or dancing." She laughed. I sat down on the couch, pulling her down next to me. Picking up her legs, I placed them in my lap.

"Wh-wha-what are you doing?" she asked nervously.

"You said your feet hurt, didn't you?"

"Um yeah but—"

"What you getting into tonight after the club?" I asked, cutting her off unfastening the shoe strap from around her ankle so that I could rub her pretty feet.

"My bed." She smiled, being sarcastic. "I can't believe you're rubbing my feet right now, Jinx. This is so embarrassing."

"It's no one right here but us. Everyone is over there chilling. There's no need to be embarrassed."

"Oh god, that feels good!"

"You got any kids, Paris?"

"Nah, no kids yet."

"Do you want any?"

"Are we really discussing this right now? I can barely hear you over the loud music."

"Answer my question."

"Yes, in the future, I want kids, Jinx. Since we are asking questions, do you have any kids, a wife, or crazy baby mamas?"

"Nah, I'm single as a dollar bill, Paris."

"Stop lying, Jinx. What are the chances that you're single? This is 2019, boo."

"I'm dead ass serious. I have a few female friends that I deal with on occasions, but no one that I would call my lady."

"Oh my god, this feels so good, Jinx."

"You got some pretty ass feet." I leaned in talking in her ear over the music playing in the background."

"Thank you. Thanks for the massage. That was everything, Jinx. You have no idea how good that felt." She sat up from her comfortable position, removing her legs off my lap.

As she started putting her shoes back on, I looked up seeing Gunna on his way over to me.

"Jinx, come on, bro! I know you got a little foot fetish and all, but bro rubbing bitches feet in the club is a dub, nigga! Broooo, you playing, right?" Gunna laughed, bending over holding his stomach while laughing uncontrollably. He was being extra as fuck.

"Aye, chill the fuck out, Gunna."

"Yeah, chill the fuck out because this ain't what you want, love, trust me. I'm not going to just sit here and be too many more bitches tonight!" Paris snapped, standing to her feet. I grabbed her wrapping my arms around her waist, walking her backwards to the corner away from everyone.

"Why are you letting Gunna get to you?"

"The fact that you're standing here defending his disrespectful ass shows me exactly what type of person you are!"

"I know Gunna, so that's why I'm defending him right now."

"Well, that's the rude asshole I was telling you about. He's rude as fuck, period!"

"That's my muthafuckin' brother, so I'm always gone have his back."

"Even when he's wrong?"

"You are doing the most right now, ma. I wasn't there, so I really don't know what happened between y'all. I do know my brother, and right now, he was joking with me. Gunna is a street nigga, and unfortunately, bitch is one of his favorite words."

"So you are justifying the disrespect?"

"No, I'm saying he didn't mean it disrespectfully. That's just how he talks."

"I should've slapped his stupid ass," she huffed, folding her arms over her chest.

"His name is Gunna for a reason. That nigga will pump yo ass full of slugs over less without thinking twice about it!" I hissed through gritted teeth, before walking off.

Pulling my blunt from behind my ear, I sparked it up to calm my nerves.

Chapter Seven

PARIS

"Oh, so you're supposed to be mad now?"

"Look, just walk away ma! I don't feel like being bothered right now," he snapped, voice full of irritation.

"You know what, Jinx. I don't even know why I wasted my time!" I spat, turning to walk away. He grabbed my arm, pushing me back up against the railing overlooking the club.

"First of all, don't ever point your muthafuckin' finger in my face unless you want me to break that bitch clean off! Secondly, lower your fuckin' voice and fix your face before you walk away from me!"

"Excuse me!"

"You heard what the fuck I said! Don't think for one second just because your ass is fine as fuck that I won't snatch yo ass up. I don't know what type of niggas you're used to, but when you're dealing with a savage like me, you gone show me some fuckin' respect!"

I was speechless standing there watching his mouth move trying to figure out if I was going crazy or not. The way Jinx just talked to me had me feeling confused. I was mad about his choice of words, but at the same time, the way he just checked me had me completely turned on.

"Let my arm go," I uttered, barely above a whisper.

"Are you done acting an ass?"

"I guess so."

"I see you got your attitude together and fixed your face."

Taking his hand leading him back to the couch where we were alone, I straddled his lap. "Aye, what you doing, Paris?"

Ignoring him, I hungrily kissed his lips. I don't know what came over me, but I decided to do what felt natural. Feeling him squeezing my plump ass, I deepened the kiss.

"Let's start the night over?" I panted, breaking away from the kiss.

"Damn Paris, I'm not even no kissing ass nigga, but I ain't even mad at that kiss. Come on, let's get out of here."

"What? I can't leave just yet. It's my bestie's birthday."

"Go chill with your girls, but just know you're coming home with me tonight, Paris."

"We're not having sex. I hope you know that." He laughed, rubbing his hands together like Birdman.

"That's cool as long as you let me rub on that big booty of yours."

"Ok deal. Let me go back over here and chill with my people before they think I'm acting funny."

"Alright, but don't try to sneak off. I got your number, so don't make me pull up on you."

"See you later, Jinx." I waved, walking away.

❧

It was after one in the morning, and I was ready to call it a night. I celebrated my best friend's birthday with her, dancing, drinking, having a good time, but now it was time to go. I knew more than likely I wasn't going to be able to make it work tomorrow, and that pissed me off.

"What's wrong, Paris?"

"I'm tired, Dream. You know I worked today."

"I know, thanks for coming out. I'm drunk as hell, but I had fun tonight."

"Me too."

"If you're ready, we can get ready to head out."

"Ok, we can go. I just need to figure out where my sister went."

"She's on the dance floor downstairs. She's been avoiding Gunna all night."

"Shit, I would be too with his rude ass!"

"It's more to the story, but I'll let her tell you her business. I'll go down to get her. Be ready to leave when I get back."

"Ok Dream I'll be right here."

My phone alerted me that I had a text message.

Jinx: *Wyd?*

Me: *Waiting on my ppl so that I can leave. I'm tired."*

Jinx: *You was leaving without telling me?*

Me: *I was just about to text you, I promise.*

Jinx: *Text me your address, I'ma come scoop you up.*

Me: *Call me whenever you leave. I might be sleep if it's too late.*

Jinx: *Cool.*

I got up to see what was taking Dream so long. Walking over to the railing overlooking the club, I saw my sister standing in the middle of Gunna who was going back and forth with some other light-skinned dude. I grabbed all of our belongings running down the stairs as fast as I could. Halfway down the steps, shots rang out. I looked up to see Dream and Lundyn running towards the exit following closely behind Gunna.

By the time I made it to the bottom of the stairs, the club had erupted in total chaos, as everyone ran for the exit. When I finally made it outside, I panicked when I couldn't find Lundyn or Dream anywhere. Running through the parking lot, I frantically searched until I found my car. That's when I realized valet had my car keys. My only concern right now was making sure my sister was straight and getting to my gun inside of my car. Running over to the valet area, they had the door closed.

Bam! Bam! Bam!

I banged on the door and window till someone came to see what I wanted.

"Valet is closed, Miss.," the worker informed me.

"Look, I need the keys to my car so that I can get out of here! What the fuck you mean valet is closed?" I snapped, throwing the ticket for my keys through the slot in the window. The woman at the window retrieved my keys off the hook then slid them under the slot.

"It's not safe for the drivers to go out because they are shooting inside the club, so you're going to have to get your car yourself."

I snatched my keys then ran off shaking my head. I carefully watched my surroundings as I made my way to my car. Using my key fob when I was halfway there, I pressed the button twice to unlock and start my G-Wagon. Once I was safely inside, I locked the doors then pulled my purple .9mm from underneath the passenger seat. After a minute went by, I backed out of the parking space. Halfway to the exit of the parking lot, I spotted Jinx along with another person walking towards a yellow and blue old school Box Chevy to the left of me.

"Oh shit!" I panicked when I noticed a dark hooded figure creeping up slowly behind them. Now on alert, I removed the safety off my gun, rolling my window down in a hurry.

"Jinx, look out!" I yelled, trying to warn him of the potential danger behind him.

When the dark figure heard my voice, he raised his gun preparing to shoot. Since I had a perfect shot, I took it, emptying the entire clip in his direction.

"Got yo ass!" I hit my target, dropping him to the ground instantly.

Locking eyes with Jinx right when he was getting ready to fire his weapon at me, my heart dropped. "Ahhhhhhh don't shoot!" I screamed, hands trembling around the trigger of my smoking gun.

"Tino! Hop in my ride and pull off, and when you get to the corner, call White Boy and tell him what's up! He knows what to do."

"I got you, bro," the guy Jinx referred to as Tino ran off following instructions. I was frozen in place not able to move when I realized the person I shot wasn't moving.

"Paris, what's up with you? We gotta get the fuck up outta here now. Let's go!"

I heard Jinx talking, but I couldn't move. It felt like the wind had been knocked out of me.

"Aye slide over!"

My legs were frozen, and I couldn't move a muscle. Jinx eventually picked me up, carrying me to the back seat. After securing the seatbelt around me, he got back in my G-Wagon and pulled off.

Chapter Eight

JINX

I fucked up in a major way tonight, and it almost cost me my life. I turned my back for one second, and I got caught slipping. What really surprised me was the way Paris held me down. She straight murked whoever that pussy ass nigga was trying to get at Tino and me. She left that nigga's thoughts lying next to him on the cold pavement. There was no coming back from that shit.

After Paris realized the person she shot was dead, she went into shock. While she was mentally processing what had gone down, my main focus was on getting us the fuck up out of there. I knew for a fact that my crew would handle the situation back at the club. I had a team of niggas who handled situations like this for me to ensure tonight's events wouldn't lead back to any of us. Therefore I wasn't worried at all. The only thing I was battling with was whether or not I could trust Paris well enough to bring her to my crib.

After going back and forth with myself for a few minutes, I decided to go ahead and trust my gut instinct that was telling me I could trust her. After all, she did just kill a nigga over me. If that didn't prove how solid she was, I don't know what did.

Twenty minutes later, I pulled up outside the tall iron gates surrounding my house in San Pedro, California. Using my left hand, I placed it on the hand scanner that read my fingerprints, giving me access to enter my property. When the gate opened, I pulled inside parking along my circular driveway then got out the car.

"Paris, we are about to go inside my house. I don't know what's going on with you, but I promise I got you."

She rocked back and forth, staring off into space. Her mind was still elsewhere. I didn't even realize she was still holding the gun until her hands started trembling. After removing the purple 9mm from her hands, I made sure the safety was on then placed it behind my back. Reaching across her lap, I picked up her phone that was sitting on the seat, putting it in my pocket. Wrapping the straps from her oversized handbag around my neck, I then proceeded to carry Paris bridal style to the front door. It was a struggle, but I finally got the door to open. Once inside, I used my foot to close the door behind me.

"Hey Jinx, I saw you pull in on the monitor, so I came to meet you."

"It's too late for you to be up, Mama G. Go to bed."

"What is wrong with this young lady?" my housekeeper, Geraldine aka Mama G, asked helping me with Paris' bags.

"Mama G, do me a favor. Can you get the guest bedroom ready for my guest? When you finish, come to my room and get me. When you're done, I need you to go back to the guesthouse. I got it from here."

"It's already done, Jinx. There's fresh linen in the bathroom if she needs to shower. Also, as always, I left your plate from dinner in the microwave. I'll retire to my suite for the evening. See you tomorrow, baby."

"Thanks, Mama G, I appreciate you," I called out over my shoulder, making my way up the stairs.

When I made it to the top, I went straight to my master bedroom. I would send Paris to the guest bedroom later on once she calmed down. Laying Paris down on the bed, I sat down beside her.

"Paris, are you alright? Talk to me," I asked, pulling her body close to mine.

"I didn't mean to kill him. I just didn't want him to hurt you," she cried, turning to face me.

"Why are you riding around strapped if you scared to bust your gun, Paris?"

"I'm not scared to shoot. I just never intended to kill anyone. I carry for my protection, that's it."

"If you're carrying a pistol, then be prepared to kill a muthafucka dead when necessary. This must be your first body, so I won't go too hard on you."

"I left the scene of a murder. Oh my god, I'm going to jail!"

I shook my head trying my best not to laugh. It was hard not to because her dramatic ass began to cry again. Me never being the one to sugarcoat shit, I had to keep it a buck with her.

"First off you did what the fuck you had to do, so you need to tighten the fuck up! You saved me and the homie's life tonight. Had you not been there, we both could possibly be dead!"

"I'm a murderer!"

"So am I, welcome to the club Paris."

"What?" she asked, her face full of confusion.

"You heard me right the first time. Bottom line is you bossed the fuck up tonight, and now I'm still here to live another day."

"I'm no better than the niggas who killed Quincy and left him to die!" She kept crying lightly hitting my chest. *What did I get myself into?*

"Who the fuck is Quincy, Paris?" She went silent again, staring off into space. Immediately, I knew she had blacked out on me again.

Ring, Ring!

Patting my pocket, I pulled the phone out only to realize it was Paris' phone ringing, not mine. The name that flashed across the screen read *Baby Sis*. I answered the phone in a hurry before it went to voicemail.

"Hello."

"Ummm, who is this? Where is my sister?" a soft voice spoke into the phone.

"This is Jinx lil mama. Your sister is right here with me at my house."

"Jinx? You mean Jinx from the east side?"

"The one and only. Have we met?"

"No, but I've heard plenty of stories about you and the Savage

Boyz."

"Don't believe everything you hear and only half of what you see. Muthafuckas be out here straight cappin' on the gang."

"What is Paris doing with you? Can I talk to her, please? I hope she's not mad at me for leaving, but I didn't have a choice."

"Paris is right here, but she's not feeling good. Aye, let me ask you a question who's Quincy?"

"That's her first love. He was brutally murdered a few years back. She was there when it all went down. Why, what's going on with Paris?"

"That explains a lot. Aye, check it out. Can you send me your location to her phone? I'm about to send my brother to come get you. She keeps blacking out. I think she might need a familiar face around to bring her back to reality."

"Is she having an anxiety attack? Oh my god, now I'm worried."

"It's a little bit more to the story."

"I just sent my location to her phone. Get her to the shower and let the cold water hit her till she calms down. That always helps her to relax."

"Ok, I'm on it."

"Please look out for my sister until I get there. Something serious must've happened for her anxiety to be triggered."

"I got Paris. Let me get off this phone. I'm gone hit my brother to come scoop you up. His name is Gunna."

"Gunna, aka Martez Gates? Please tell me that's not who you're talking about."

"Damn, I guess you know everyone."

"Ugh, I can't believe Gunna is your brother. I know his rude ass very well. He just dropped me off at home not too long ago."

"That's even better. That way, the ride to my house won't be awkward between y'all."

"Let me go roll me a blunt. I'm going to need to be high in order to take this ride," she huffed into the phone.

"Be looking out for his call. I'm gone send your number to him. He already knows your address."

"I guess it's cool." Lundyn sighed before hanging up the phone.

Chapter Nine

LUNDYN

I had no idea what was going on with my sister, but I was on my way to make sure she was ok. I was surprised to learn Paris was with Jinx but happy to know that she was safe. When Jinx let me know he was sending Gunna to pick me up, my heart dropped to the pit of my stomach. I instantly felt overwhelmed with emotions knowing there was only one Gunna in Cali that he could be talking about. It was awkward enough riding in the car with him after he possibly killed the guy I was dancing with in the club. Now this time was different because we would be alone, and I didn't know if my heart could take the emotional turmoil that I felt brewing inside of me.

Gunna and I went way back. We actually went to high school together for a little while before he dropped out. During that time, we grew close and became really good friends. Then one day he switched up on me. Other than the few times at parties or in traffic, I hadn't seen much of him before tonight.

After I finished getting dressed, I checked my appearance in the full body mirror in my bedroom. I was still cute even though I had changed clothes after I came home from the club. I dressed down in a red Champion jogger set. However, my body was still looking right. My frame was slim thick, but I had a big booty and wide hips that all the niggas loved. My long hair was pulled into a high ponytail to the side, showing off my bare fresh face. I applied a little gloss to my lips then went to the living room to wait on my ride.

323-555-1212: *I'm outside.*

Me: *Coming out now, give me two minutes.*

Gunna was still on that same bullshit he was on when he dropped me off earlier. He didn't even have the decency to call me. I picked up the bag with a change of clothes for my sister, set the alarm, then made my way outside. I couldn't believe this fool was outside at three forty-five in the morning blasting my favorite Meek Mill's album *Dreams and Nightmares* like it was the daytime.

"Damn Gunna, can you cut that shit down? You probably done woke up all of my neighbors playing this loud ass music this time of morning!" I snapped, opening the car door with an attitude.

"Man shut the fuck up and get yo big head ass in the car so that I can pull off. You ain't even got in the car yet good and you already talkin' shit, Lundyn!"

"That music is loud as hell! I live in a nice, quiet neighborhood. Turn that shit down!"

"Nigga, this is Gardena. You're just two lights and one stop sign away from the hood. Muthafuckas kill me acting like they live in Calabasas or some shit because they move to Gardena or Carson. Yo ass is still in the ghetto, and it damn sure ain't no Kardashian's around this bitch!"

"Please just get me to my sister. We don't have to say shit else to each other."

"You still mad at a nigga after all this time, I see." Gunna laughed, mushing me in the face.

"Stop playing with me, damn. I swear I can't stand your stupid ass."

For the rest of the ride, I sat quietly staring out of the window collecting my thoughts. I hated the way Gunna had the ability to make me feel vulnerable. The last thing I wanted was for him to mistake my love for him as weakness.

It took less than twenty minutes for us to reach our destination. I couldn't believe the big beautiful house we pulled up in front of. The house was super dope. Tall iron gates surrounded it, and it had a beautiful ocean front view that I instantly fell in love with.

"I love this house!" I expressed, looking around in awe.

"Quit acting like a groupie and get ready to get out the car, big head." Gunna placed his hand on what looked like a scanner, and the gate slowly opened.

"This house is dope as fuck! It's huge like my childhood home."

"Wait till you see the inside. Come on, let's go."

"Can you get my bag, please?"

"Hell no! Do I look like the fuckin' help to you?"

"Never mind, Gunna," I said, snatching the bag of clothes from the back seat. I slammed the door real hard being petty just to piss him off.

"Don't be slamming my shit, Lundyn!" He mushed me again then ran to the front door unlocking it.

When I stepped inside the house, I was blown away. The high ceilings and wall to wall windows had a nice beautiful view of the ocean.

"This house is so beautiful, Gunna."

"Have a seat and let me go find Jinx."

"My sister is with him, so I'm coming with you."

"Just come on and don't touch shit."

"I'm not a child, Gunna I don't need you telling me what to do."

Rolling my eyes, I followed his irritating ass up the double winding staircase. I couldn't help staring at all the different paintings on the wall. The décor was black and white with a pop of red, giving the house a *Scarface* type of vibe. We entered the master suite, and my mouth hit the floor. The bedroom was big enough to be a one-bedroom apartment. In graffiti writing, there was a huge mural on the wall that read *SAVAGE LIFE*. The bed was probably the size of two king-size beds put together. In the middle of me being mesmerized by the bedroom, I noticed Jinx cradling my sister in his arms while she slept like a baby. He was being so gentle with her running his hand up and down her back to soothe her.

"Hi, I'm Lundyn. You must be Jinx." I waved at him with a big smile on my face.

"Sup ma, I finally got your sister to calm down. She just fell asleep about ten minutes ago."

"That cold shower did the trick, didn't it?"

"Yeah, it took her a couple of minutes, but she was finally able to calm herself down."

"It looks like I came all this way for nothing. Thank you for taking care of Paris in my absence. Let me wake her up so that we can get going."

"We probably should just let her rest till the morning. Since you came all this way, you can stay in one of the guest rooms for the night."

"Are you sure? I don't want to invade your personal space."

"Jinx, I got it from here bro," Gunna interrupted us. "I'll set her big head ass up for the night in one of the guest rooms. I'm tired as a muthafucka my damn self."

"Good looking out, G. I'll see y'all first thing in the morning. One more thing do you know if White Boy took care of that?"

"You should already know he handled it, bro," he replied, as I followed Gunna out the bedroom.

"I thought you were taking me to the guest bedrooms?"

"I will in a minute. Let's go put one in the air first."

"Gunna, no, I'm tired. Did you forget y'all got me up out of my warm bed at almost four in the morning, to come all this way for nothing. Right now, I just wanna go to sleep. I'm drunk, and I'm tired. Plus, I had a long day at the shop. Then I had to deal with you acting a fool in the club tonight. Please, I just want to go lay down."

"It won't take long, I promise. Stop acting like you don't wanna smoke with a nigga. We used to do shit like this together all the time— once upon a time."

"That was then, and this is now. Back then, you were different."

"I'm still the same. Ain't nothing changed, but my pockets got fatter."

"Let's just go so that we can get this over with!" I spat. "Please don't think I'm impressed because you got a little money now."

"Are you done? You got a whole lot of shit to say for someone who not impressed." He laughed, mushing me in the face again as we walked outside on the deck that was overlooking the water.

Gunna's childish antics no longer mattered to me when I finally took in the breathtaking view. The temperature was pleasant outside with a slight breeze.

"It's nice out here even though it's kind of windy."

"I love chilling out here. It's peaceful."

"Yeah, I don't blame you. I could probably sit out here and meditate for hours. This shit is a vibe."

"What's up with you?"

"What do you mean what's up with me?"

"Stop acting crazy Lundyn, man fuck!"

"Don't yell at me, fool!"

"Look, I'm just trying to see what you been up to?"

"Other than working at Ty's Beauty Bar doing hair and makeup, I be at home or living my best life."

"You work there? My barber is next door to that salon. I'm surprised I've never seen you up there."

"I have a suite in the back, so most of the time I come and go through the back door. I didn't know you and Jinx were brothers."

"We're not brothers by blood, but we are definitely family. Jinx has been down since the day I met him when I was eight years old."

"Oh, y'all grew up together?"

"We lived in the same group home growing up."

"I asked because he said you were his brother when I talked to him earlier. You never mentioned your family in the past, so I had no idea."

"Back in the day, we were too busy cutting class and getting high together, that's why." He laughed, pulling me close to him.

"That's so true," I smiled at the memory. "We used to have the best conversations. Well, until you switched up on me." I sighed before pulling away from him.

"I never switched up on you Lundyn."

"Yeah, you did. You changed overnight, and that shit hurt me so bad."

"Lundyn, come here man." He tried hugging me, but I snatched away.

"Stop Gunna, I can't do this right now," I turned trying to walk away from him.

"You not about to go nowhere until you finish telling me what's on your mind."

"You want to know how bad you hurt me? No problem, I'll tell you, since you never gave me a chance to. When you switched up on me, it hurt because you knew my parents were sentenced to do all that time in the Feds. I felt lost, and I needed you to be there for me, the same way I had been there for you. I couldn't talk to my sister because she was already under enough pressure. Honestly, all I had was you to confide in Martez Gates, and you weren't there for me!" I screamed as tears threaten to fall down my face.

"Don't be calling me by my birth name, ma. You know I hate my name because of who it's connected to. I don't ever want to hear Martez Gates come out of your mouth again. I can't even believe you still remember it."

"I remember everything about you. The way you laugh, the way you smell, the way you run your hands over your waves when your upset. Why would I forget?"

"It's been a minute since we last saw each other, Lun."

"I know, but you never forget about someone you care about no matter how much time has passed by."

"You're trying to gas a nigga head up I see." He laughed.

"No, I'm just being honest, Gunna."

"How are your parents doing by the way?" he inquired, changing the subject.

"Still locked up. Hopefully, they will be paroled soon. I really miss them both so much.

"I miss yo big head ass, you looking real good, ma."

"Don't lie. You don't miss me."

"I don't waste time telling lies. You should know that about me. What's up with you? Why are you trippin' on me right now?"

"Don't play dumb nigga. I just poured my heart out to you just a few minutes ago, and you brushed me off. I need you to tell me what did I ever do to you? Please help me to understand why you cut me off when I did nothing to deserve that, and you know it."

"Woah, are you serious right now?"

"Yes, I'm serious! I know I wasn't your girlfriend, but I thought we at least had a special bond."

"Damn Lundyn, I just wanted to come out here to ease my mind. Why did you have to get emotional on a nigga? Man, fuck!"

"Because I'm an emotional person! Do you know how awkward it is for me being around you knowing that the last time I saw you, before today, you walked away from me right after I told you I had feelings for you. You left and never spoke to me again."

"I was heavy in the streets Lundyn, and no matter how much I fucked with you, I couldn't let you get caught up in my bullshit."

"That's just an excuse, and you know it. Did you forget who my father was? Street shit is nothing new to me."

"Here, hit this so you can calm yo fuckin' nerves."

He passed me the blunt clearly agitated, but I didn't care. I gladly accepted it taking two deep pulls, before walking over to the end of the deck to gather myself. I hated opening up to people leaving myself feeling vulnerable.

Wrapping his arms around my waist, minutes later, Gunna whispered in my ear, "Lundyn listen. If I hurt you, then I apologize. That was never my intention. Truth be told, you're the only chick I would ever rock with on some real love type shit. I still fuck with you, and I honestly just want to see you happy."

"Even if I'm happy with someone else?"

"Man gone somewhere with that shit, Lundyn!" he said, releasing me. "Hell no, I don't want you with no one else. I realized that tonight."

"Stop lying to me."

"Fuck I'ma lie for, Lun?"

"Because that's what niggas do— lie, lie, lie!" I rambled on and on.

"I swear to God you gone make me fuck yo ass up, Lundyn! You know a nigga don't like expressing himself and shit, and you got me out here feeling like I need to go change my tampon with the shit you on right now. I already said how I feel. I fucks with you. If I ever marry a bitch, it's gone be you. That's why I reacted the way I did when I saw you let that nigga push all up on you tonight." Gunna snapped, backing me up against the railing on the deck.

"I was just dancing. You overreacted and ruined the entire night. I'm serious about what I said just so you know. Someone else is gone come along and lock my fine ass down." I shrugged, turning my head to look away from his angered expression.

I didn't know why, but I was fighting back tears. He had my emotions all over the place, and I hated it. Gunna turned my head to face him. "Lundyn, stop fucking playing with me. You should already know what it is," he hissed, close enough to my face that I could feel his heart beating out of his chest.

"Uhmmmm," I released an involuntary moan as he placed his soft lips on top of mine, while both of his hands were wrapped around my neck. The kiss was so intense that my knees felt weak.

"Don't be mad at a nigga, Lun. I have my reasons why I did what I did."

"I miss you in my life, Gunna," I confessed, before deepening our kiss.

Everything about this moment felt so right. The feeling of his hands roaming around my body had me on fire. When Gunna slid his hands under my shirt cupping my breasts, I decided to pull back.

"Ca c-can you please show me to the guest bedroom?"

"What's wrong now, Lundyn?" He backed up, running his hands over his waves.

"I'm not trying to play myself again. I'm already feeling vulnerable as it is, please show me to the guest room."

"I will. Just stay out here with me a few more minutes. Let a nigga enjoy you for a little while longer ma."

"Two more minutes that's it, and no more kissing."

Chapter Ten

PARIS

"Lundyn, I don't know how many times I gotta tell you about smoking in the damn house," I said to myself as the strong scent of marijuana mixed with the heat from the sun shining down on me and woke me up from the best sleep I've had in a very long time.

"My bad ma, I figured if you could drool on a nigga's chest half the night, I should at least be able to smoke a little Kush first thing in the morning."

When I heard a voice that I didn't recognize, I jumped up and opened my eyes to check my surroundings. After blinking a few times to make sure I wasn't tripping, I gave a nervous smile, not sure where I was, or how I even got here. Luckily, I recognized who I was with. That still didn't explain why I was with Jinx.

"Umm, this is awkward. How did we get here? We didn't um.... you know have sex?"

"Stop playing with me, Paris. You don't remember what happened last night at Club Reign?"

"No, the last thing I remember is walking to my car. I know for a fact I was alone when I left." I sighed, closing my eyes to replay last night's events over in my head. "Oh my god!" I yelled, sitting up when it finally registered in my brain what Jinx meant. "I...I killed someone," immediately I started to feel like shit. "Jinx, I feel terrible about what happened last night."

"Please don't black out on me again like you did last night. It was all bad.

"I blacked out?"

"Hell yeah, you did! If it weren't for your sister calling your phone when she did, telling me how to calm you down, I probably would have had to call 9-1-1."

"Wait, you talked to my sister? Is she ok? I should strangle her ass for leaving me last night."

"Yeah, I sent my brother to pick her up late last night, but by the time she made it here you had fallen asleep already."

"So, she went back home?"

"Nah, I let her stay in one of the guest rooms overnight."

"I can't believe the events of last night. Should I be worried?"

"Listen, ma. What happened last night can't leave this room. The only people who know what happened are you, me, and my fam who was there with me. Well, Gunna knows too, but you can trust him. I expect you to keep your mouth shut unless you plan on going to jail. Don't even tell your sister when you get downstairs. Just tell her you were robbed if she asks. I need you to stay focused. Don't tell anyone what happened, is that understood?"

"I would never put my freedom in jeopardy, but I want you to know my sister is trustworthy."

"That's up to you. If you trust her with your life, that's your decision."

"I do trust her. Do you know if there were any surveillance cameras, and what happened to the body?"

"After you left, I sent my crew to clean up the mess. There aren't any traces of a murder and no footage of the shooting taking place last night."

"How can you be sure?"

"I may have fucked up last night, but my crew stays on point!"

"I guess that leaves me with no choice other than to trust your word. Why am I naked wrapped in nothing but a sheet?"

"You blacked out. I told you that already. Your sister said to put you in a cold shower, so that's what I did," he shrugged. "She left a bag with a change of clothes for you on the chair by the door."

"Thanks, Jinx. I appreciate you for being a gentleman and taking care of me last night."

"No problem. It felt good having your fine ass laid up with a nigga last night. We have to have another sleepover real soon." He said, giving me a sexy grin before getting out of bed.

"Something smells good, do you smell that?"

"Yeah, that's probably Mama G hooking up some breakfast for me."

"Your mother lives here?"

"I'm an orphan, ma. I don't got no mother."

"What?"

"Just go put something on so that we can go eat breakfast."

Deciding to drop the conversation, I got out of bed. After handling my hygiene, I went downstairs to the dining room searching for Jinx. I was shocked to find Lundyn sitting at the table eating breakfast with Jinx and Gunna. A petite middle age woman with long, gray curly hair walked in the dining room to serve me breakfast. Looking at the different assortment of food left my mouth watering. I couldn't remember the last time I'd eaten a southern breakfast. There was smothered potatoes, shrimp and grits, fried catfish, fried chicken and waffles, salmon patties, scrambled eggs, and fresh fruit laid out buffet style on the table.

"Good morning, everyone." I smiled, taking a seat next to my sister.

"Paris, this is my bro Gunna. Let's start this morning off right," Jinx properly introduced us, but I still wasn't impressed.

"Sup, ma?" Gunna laughed then went back to eating his food. Lundyn hugged me because her mouth was too stuffed with food to talk.

"Good morning, young lady, I'm Mama G. I hope you're hungry because I'm about to hook you up a plate."

"Thanks, Mama G, I'm starving."

"I thought you would be hungry this morning. That's why I

decided to get up early and make a big meal. I know you and my boy over there had a long night." She smiled, piling my plate with food.

"Come on Mama G. We didn't even do shit last night!" Jinx laughed, shaking his head. Picking up the champagne flute in front of me, I drank my mimosa down in one gulp.

"Oh my Lord, are you nervous dear? Let me get you another drink. Eat some food, baby." Mama G smiled, walking off to get me another mimosa. I said a silent prayer over my food then dug into my plate.

"How did you end up here with, Jinx?" Lundyn inquired, being nosey as usual.

"I was robbed coming out the club last night, he saved me," I lied, pointing at Jinx.

"Oh my god, Paris! I'm sorry that happened to you. I feel so bad that I was forced to leave you by yourself. That one fuck up could have cost you your life."

"I'm fine, sis, relax."

"Let me go outside to get some air." She sighed, standing up from the table. Lundyn walked off with Gunna trailing close behind her.

After I finished eating breakfast, I went out on the deck to clear my head. These last twenty-four hours have been crazy.

"Paris, can I talk to you for a minute?" Jinx asked, walking up behind me.

"Umm...sure what's up?"

"Spend the day with me?"

"You want to spend the day with me?"

"Ain't that what I just said?" He laughed, placing both of his hands around my waist. "Let me take you out. We can go shopping, out to lunch, or dinner. Shit, it doesn't matter. I just want to spend some time with you. I want to show you my appreciation for basically saving my life last night."

"Somebody lost a son, and a child could have possibly lost their dad because of me. I'm really not in the mood to shop or do anything else. I feel awful about what happened Jinx."

"You did what the fuck you had to do. That nigga was a liability, and now he's no longer a threat to me. I will owe you as long as I have breath in my body Paris, whether you like it or not."

"If anything, I would love just to get away to clear my head. I'm not in the mood to shop."

"Let's go then. I know the perfect spot where you can clear your mind."

"I can't, not now at least. I already missed work today. I was supposed to do a surprise home visit early this morning."

"Alright, that's cool. We can postpone it, but I'll be at your house when you get off work next Friday, and you'll be mine for the weekend, Paris."

"How do you know I don't already have plans?"

"If you have plans, cancel them. I got your address, so don't think you can dodge my ass either."

"I will still need to go home, take another shower, and change clothes after work."

"This sounds like just another excuse. What time do you get off?"

"Around three o'clock on Fridays, why?"

"I'll be there to pick you up at about five o'clock. That should give you enough time to go home and do whatever it is that you females like to do when you get home from work." He smiled, kissing me on the cheek.

"I guess we can go, Jinx. Five o'clock is a perfect time. Please don't be late. Let me text you my address."

"I told you that I already got your address. Did you think I was playing?"

"I sure did."

"No offense but you and your sister slept in my crib last night. I did a quick background check to make sure you both checked out. You can never be too sure nowadays."

"No offense taken. I think I should get ready to head out now. Can I have my keys so that I can go?"

"Yes, let me go upstairs and get them. I'll be right back."

Twenty minutes later, I was in my car on my way home alone. Gunna insisted that he take Lundyn to the house, and I snuck off deciding to let them figure it out on their own after listening to them argue back and forth for ten minutes straight. Since I missed work this morning, I planned to spend the rest of my day relaxing to clear my head. Jinx wanted to take me away next weekend, so I needed to mentally prepare myself for it. In just one night, I had already killed a man to protect Jinx, and that had me feeling some type of way. The way he was able to get me worked up during that private dance let me know I was more than attracted to him. He had the potential to have me completely open, and I wasn't sure I was ready for that just yet.

Ring! Ring! My phone began to ring over the cars Bluetooth system. Not recognizing the number, I answered on the second ring.

"Hello."

"This is Global Tel-link, you have a collect call from Adonis Monroe, an inmate at a Federal Detention Center in Victorville, California. Will you accept the charges?"

"Yes, I'll accept the charges." *I wonder why my dad is calling me collect. Something must've happened because he usually calls from his cell phone,* I thought as the call connected.

"Your call is connected."

"Hello!"

"Hey dad, how are you? Is everything alright?"

"What's going on, firstborn? I'm still the same, trying to keep my head above water."

"That's good to hear." I smiled, excited to hear my dad's voice.

"They can't hold a nigga down forever."

"I know, dad. Your time is almost up. I miss you and mom so much every day."

"I miss you too, princess. Listen I'm calling to talk to you real quick."

"What is it, dad? I'm listening."

"The warden had the C.O.'s come and get me this morning to go before the parole board."

"Why? I thought that your appointment wasn't until next Tuesday. Lundyn and I made plans to drive out there to support you."

"I thought the same thing, but it was today."

"Well, what happened, how did it go?" I asked, anxiously waiting for his response.

"I don't think it went too good. I know they're going to deny my parole once again. It's fucked up, but what can I do about it?"

"Oh no! I just knew this time they would finally release you. It's been years dad. This is some bullshit. Have you heard anything from mom yet?"

"No not yet, but I believe her appointment is still next week. She's been doing everything right, staying out of trouble, so I'm sure she won't get the same decision. The Feds have been fuckin' us over for years now. I'm sick of it."

"Yeah, I know, I'm so sorry, dad."

"Don't be. It's going to be ok, princess. I'm trying to figure out my next move as we speak."

"Let me know if you need my help with anything, as always, you know I got your back."

"I will, princess. Listen the other reason why I'm calling is because I need you to come visit me before the month is up. I need a huge favor from you, but we have to talk about this in person.

"Ok Lundyn and I will come as soon as I have some free time."

"No! I want you to come by yourself Paris whenever you do decide to come. I know you're busy working that good job making all that money, but don't forget about your pops."

"Are you sure everything is alright dad? You're making me nervous."

"I'm positive, but listen, I have to get off this phone. Make sure you come down here to see me before the end of the month. I love you, princess."

"I love you too, dad. You take care of yourself."

"I will. Tell Lundyn I love her. I have to go, Paris."

"Ok, I will, dad. I'll see you soon."

Click!

Chapter Eleven

JINX

One Week Later

Growing up on the east side of Los Angeles, right in the heart of the ghetto, I've seen and done it all. When I started out here running recklessly in the streets, I was just a young little nigga. By the age of thirteen, I had already hit my first lick looking for a quick come up, and it's been on ever since. It started with me breaking in houses around the neighborhood. When that got old, I started robbing dope boyz from the west side. Where I'm from robbing muthafuckas was frowned upon, but back then I literally had nothing, so I had to get out and get it by any means necessary. I didn't have any other choice.

I was forced into a world where killings, drug dealing, and robbing was the norm, and other than playing ball, gang banging was the only way of life. My home life was dysfunctional as fuck. With no father in my life and a dope fiend mother who never wanted me, shit was hard out here.

My grandmother Naomi had to take me in at birth since my mother chose the streets and heroin over motherhood. She raised me as her own up until the day she died when I was thirteen years old. I ended up in the foster care system after her death, and that's when my life went from bad to worse. I quickly learned that this was a cold, fucked up world. Nobody ever gave me shit. That's one of the main reasons why when I first started getting money, I took everything I had by force.

By the age of sixteen, I had saved up enough money from hitting licks to buy twenty pounds of the best Cali Kush from this Jamaica cat named Hussle Man. He couldn't believe it took me less than a week to come back to him for more product, so he doubled my next shipment for the low. I was no dummy, and I knew I needed a team, so I brought a few of my brothers in from the group home to put money in their pockets. I formed a crew called the Savage Boyz, and it's been on ever since. It took me a little over a year to make my first million dollars and get the respect I felt like I deserved in the streets. Niggas thought I was a joke because the real money is in selling bricks of cocaine, but that wasn't my thing. My mama was a fiend, and I refused to help keep flooding the streets with that bullshit. I got out there and grind 24/7. I kept my foot on these niggas necks, and they had no choice but to respect me. Now with the way laws have changed, I have four marijuana dispensaries on the east side near my traps that bring in millions of dollars in profit the legal way. I use the income from my dispensaries to cover my ass in case I ever get jammed by the Feds.

When I hit the block on 94th and Main Street, I shook my head when I spotted Devon, a kid who reminded me of my younger self, hanging around the spot serving fiends right out in the open. I've told this little nigga over and over again that this street shit wasn't for him, but he just wouldn't listen. I parked about two houses down from the trap then hopped out my ride to go holla at him.

"What's up, Jinx?"

"Shit, you tell me? I was getting ready to make my rounds till I saw yo hardheaded ass out here."

"Here you go."

You already know what I'm about to say, little nigga!" Laughing, I put Devon in a headlock. "Why yo ass ain't at school, D? I thought I told you to stay off the block, especially during school hours!" I released him waiting for an answer.

"If I'm at school and not out here, how the fuck is my brother and sister supposed to eat dinner tonight? My mama ain't been home in a week. The little money I made out here the other day, I had to pay the bills with it and put food in the house."

I knew he was telling the truth, and the shit was sad. I wasn't mad at Devon's hustle that's why I didn't let anybody fuck with him for selling on my corners. The S Boyz knew Devon was off limits and not to fuck with him unless it was approved by me first. I actually respected the fact he got out and did what he had to do to take care of his little brother and sister. I just saw more for Devon's life, and that's why I never put him on myself. I knew he had it in him to be more than just another street nigga like me.

Devon could play ball better than Kobe Bryant in his prime, and if he stayed in school, I know for a fact he has exactly what it takes to make it to the league. He didn't have to take the same route I took, and if I could help it, then I'm gone make sure he doesn't.

"Here take this and go home!" I peeled off five one-hundred-dollar bills handing it to Devon.

"Jinx I can't keep taking handouts from you. I'd rather get out here and try to make it on my own, big bro."

"Nigga take this money and get yo ass off the block. I keep telling you the streets don't love nobody, not even me."

"Jinx, I promise I'll get the money back to you bro."

"Just take yo ass to school and stay off these corners. How about this D, from now on every week you go to school without missing any days, plus keep your grades up, I'll give you a stack every Friday."

"What! Are you serious?"

"Come on lil bro, when have you ever known me to be a liar? I'm dead ass!"

"Well, you got a deal," he smiled, giving me pound.

"Alright bet, now get up out of here and go home. Bang my line if you need me."

"Later Jinx, thank you so much bro."

"You're welcome little bro, now get out of here."

When he walked off, all I could do was smile. It made me feel good that I was finally in a position to help someone knowing all the crazy shit I've done in life. Devon was a good kid he was just dealt a fucked up hand in life. His father was killed a few years back, and his mother started partying with her friends on a daily basis. She eventually developed a nasty cocaine habit and began neglecting her motherly duties. Devon, being the oldest at fourteen years old, had to pick up his mother's slack. That's why whenever I saw him on the block, I made sure to look out for him. That's something I wish someone would have done for me when I was his age out here moving recklessly. Had someone been looking out for me, there probably wouldn't have been so much bloodshed over the years, but that's a story for another day.

Walking into the trap, I instantly saw red. Not only was this nigga Tino getting his dicked sucked on the couch right out in the open, but these other niggas who were supposed to be working were sitting around shooting the shit like there wasn't a whole bitch on her knees with dick down her throat right next to them.

"Aye Tino, what the fuck is you doing nigga? Get this bitch up out the trap before I kill her smut ass!" You muthafuckas are supposed to be chasing the bag, not chasing ass!"

"We on break, boss." Red, who was one of my runners, laughed as if he was a fuckin' comedian, but I didn't find shit funny.

Walking behind the bar in the corner of the room, I poured myself a shot of D'Ussé. After throwing my shot back, I took another, then reached behind my back for my pistol. After having two more shots and seeing Red still laughing, I removed the safety sending a single shot across the room, hitting him between the eyes. His head popped like a watermelon splattering on Tino and Solo's face.

"Yooooo Jinx, what the fuck!" Tino jumped up, wiping the oozing brain matter and blood off his face with his shirt.

"Since that nigga wanted to go on break, he can stay there permanently!" I roared. "You fucking up, Tino! I gave you a promotion less than a month ago, and this is the first shit I see when I pull up to the trap?"

"It wasn't even what it looked like."

"So I didn't see you getting yo dicked sucked when I walked through the fuckin' door nigga?" I hissed, turning my head to the side looking at his goofy ass.

"Yeah bu—"

"But nothing, nigga! I don't want to hear your fucking excuses. You supposed to be running the trap making sure this bitch is boomin'. The only thing I need for you to do is keep this muthafucka stocked with product and plenty of clientele! I see I'm gone have to have White Boy put up surveillance in this spot just like he did in the rest of my traps. Y'all are not about to be fucking up and doing dumb shit on my time! Do I not pay you good? Are you not eating well off my empire, nigga?"

"My bad boss, real shit, I fucked up, and it won't happen again."

"It better not happen again or the next time it's gone cost you your fuckin' life! I don't care how much I fuck with you, my money better be right, or that's yo ass nigga on God!"

"You got my word, Jinx!"

"Shut the trap down and move everything over on 98th Street. Send the cleanup boyz to clean this shit up now." The front door opened, and Gunna walked in. "Aye, lock that door nigga!"

"Yo what the fuck happened in here, bro? Is that Red with his dome lying next to him?" He laughed, passing me a lit blunt after locking the door.

"Red is on break indefinitely." I shrugged, passing him the weapon that I used to kill Red. "Get rid of this for me, and then hit me later on. I'm about to go home to change clothes. I need you to go check up on the spot on 84th Street."

"I got you bro be safe."

After exchanging a brotherly hug with Gunna, I left heading back home to shower and get rid of the clothes that I was wearing. Red had me fucked up. I took him laughing at my seriousness as a sign of disrespect. Disrespect wasn't tolerated, especially when directed at me—period.

Chapter Twelve

PARIS

One Week Later

"Paris, stop making a big deal out of nothing. It's just a quick weekend getaway. I promise you will have a good time. You deserve this," Lundyn tried to convince me, but I wasn't sold on the idea yet.

"Maybe we should wait a little longer before we start going away for weekends. I don't want Jinx to feel like I'm just another sack chaser because that's not me at all."

"We both know that you're not a sack chaser, and once you spend some alone time with Jinx, he will too. Stop thinking of what could go wrong, and focus on what could go right."

"I'm trying, sis." I sighed, falling back on my bed. "I don't have anything to wear, and I need to pack an overnight bag."

"I knew you would say that, so that's why I picked you out a few things while you were in the shower. Your outfit for today is put to the side, and everything else is packed waiting right there by the door."

"Oh Lord, please don't have me one of your freak hoe Fashion Nova sets laid out for me to wear today. I'll pass boo." I fell out laughing at the thought.

"Don't do me like that, sis. Paris, look on the chair over there and see what I picked out. It's super cute."

Walking over to the chair, I was impressed with what Lundyn had chosen for me to wear. It was some distressed denim jeans, a coral colored lace bodysuit with a long, floral cardigan. This was exactly the look I was going for, sexy but casual at the same time. I have the perfect shoes to match, and I would accessorize for that extra pop.

"This is perfect, sis. I guess I'm going out after all."

"Good make sure you bring me something back since I heard he wants to take you shopping." She laughed, getting up off my bed. "Hurry up and get dressed so that I can curl your hair in beach wave curls."

"Thanks, sister, I'll be right back.

🐚

An hour later, I sat in my living room waiting on Jinx to pull up. He called about thirty minutes ago to let me know he was in route to my house.

"Lundyn, sit down. Let's talk until Jinx gets here."

"Oh Lord, you must be trying to get in my business since you don't have any."

"Yep, all in your business." I laughed, patting the seat on the couch next to me.

"What do you want to know, nosey?"

"You and Jinx's brother, Gunna, seemed pretty cozy yesterday. What was up with that?"

"Don't even bring him up. He has been driving me crazy. Don't you remember him we went to school together?"

"Nah I don't remember him. He must be the one who kept your ass in detention. Is he that friend?"

"Yep, that's the one." She laughed. "Anyway, at one point we were really close, then the next we weren't even speaking." She sighed, looking away.

"What happened between y'all?"

"Nothing happen, that's why I was completely caught off guard when he stopped talking to me. I did have a chance to ask him about it the night we stayed over Jinx's house."

"Ok, and what did he say?"

"He said he was in the streets too heavy and didn't want me to get caught up, but I say it's bullshit."

"What makes you think that?"

"I opened up to him and told him I had feelings for him. Shortly after, he stopped coming around."

"That's fucked up sis, I'm sorry. Why didn't you tell me any of this when it was happening?"

"Because you had enough pressure on you, and I didn't want to add my small problems to the list."

"We are sisters. I'll be there for you anytime you need me. I don't care what I'm dealing with just say the word."

"I know that already, and that's why I chose to just deal with it alone."

"So, when was the last time you saw Gunna before the night when we were all at Jinx's house?"

"I've seen him a few times in random places in the last few years, but it was hella awkward."

"Do you still have feelings for him?"

"Honestly the way I care for Gunna will never change. I know he's been through a lot in his childhood and that probably has him scared to love."

"I wouldn't be surprised, Lundyn. I work with children of all ages every day, and sometimes the trauma they endure scars them for life. If you ever get the chance again, tell him how you feel. If he doesn't feel the same, then you know how to move going forward."

Ding Dong!

"That's probably Jinx at the door. I'm gonna head to my room so that you can have some privacy. Have fun, Paris. I love you."

"Love you too, Lundyn. I promise to call you later."

"Good because I want all the tea."

"Girl bye!" I laughed, pulling the front door open.

"Damn ma, I didn't think you could get any prettier, but I guess I was wrong. You look good!"

"Thanks, Jinx, come in."

Smiling, I stepped aside. I couldn't get over how handsome he was.

Standing over six feet tall, chocolate brown skin, with a muscular build, dark, mysterious eyes and long thick beard that was neatly trimmed had me damn near drooling at the mouth, not to mention the way he smelled. Oh my god, I loved whatever cologne he wore, and even though his Versace jeans were slightly hanging off his ass, it didn't take away from his sexiness. Jinx's energy screamed he was a boss ass nigga, and I loved that shit!

"Why you got that goofy look on your face, Paris? You ready to head out?" he asked, pulling me in for a hug. "Fuck, you smell good. What kind of perfume is that? It's my new favorite scent."

"You're so crazy." Laughing, I playfully hit his chest. "It's Chanel, and thank you. I love compliments. I was thinking about how good you look as well. That's why I was staring at you like that."

"Oh, you were checking a nigga out?" He smirked, looking down at me.

"I guess you could say that." Smiling, I pulled back from him.

"Your house is nice, ma. Do you live here by yourself?"

"Nah, Lundyn lives with me. She just went to her room. Let me go grab my sweater so that we can go."

"It's cool ma, take your time."

After locking up the house, we headed outside to Jinx's car. Today he was driving a late model Chevy. After opening the passenger door for me, he walked around to get inside.

"Do you have a thing for old school cars?"

"I only drive old school Chevys. You should see my collection in my garage."

"That's dope, Jinx. Most guys like to drive them expensive ass foreign cars."

"I'm not like most niggas, P. I don't ride the wave. I create my own wave. Foreign cars bring too much attention to you. I like to be low-key. Besides these old school cars cost money to run good like this. My cars all have custom made V-12 engines, and the best paint jobs and sound systems inside of them. This car cost me about seventy-five stacks to get customized to my liking."

"I bet, this car is dope inside and out. Where are we headed to?"

"It's a surprise. Sit back and let me take care of you for at least the next twenty-four hours."

"I can't lie, Jinx. I'm nervous."

"Don't be. Just relax, sit back, and enjoy the ride. I promise I got you, Paris."

For the next hour, we made small talk while riding on the freeway. I didn't know where we were headed, but I was looking forward to the long ride and quick getaway now.

Hours Later

Checking the time on my iPhone, it was 10:11 p.m. When Jinx woke me up, I didn't even realize that I had fallen asleep. When I noticed the flashing sign that read *Welcome To Las Vegas*, my mouth dropped.

"Did you really bring me here?" I screamed in excitement. "I haven't been to Vegas since my sixteenth birthday."

"Oh yeah?"

"Yeah, my dad flew my best friend Dream and me out, and we had the time of our lives."

"How old are you now?"

"I'm twenty-five my birthday is March eighteenth."

"No shit! We're the same age, and my birthday is March sixteenth. That's crazy."

"I know right, Pisces gang!" I laughed, as we cruised down the Las Vegas strip.

The streets were lit up from the many different hotels. The sidewalks were packed with tourist sightseeing and taking pictures of the glamorous hotels.

"You made it out here fast, Jinx."

"It took just a little under six hours."

"I can't believe I slept through most of the ride. I would have really enjoyed looking at the scenery."

"You were sleeping so good that I didn't want to wake you. I figured you must have been tired."

"I guess I was and didn't even realize it. Working the club at night and then getting up to go to work first thing the next morning was beginning to take a toll on me."

"Well, that part of your life is over, ma. Just focus on your nine-to-five." He pulled into the valet parking at the Bellagio Hotel. "Come on, Paris. Let's get out so that we can check in. It's late as fuck. Check in was hours ago."

"Ok, let's head inside."

After checking in, we found the elevator riding up to the top floor. He booked the presidential suite, so I already knew the room was nice. He had a special key card that allowed us access to the floor the suite was on. When the elevator stopped, the door opened, and we entered the suite.

"Now that I'm of age, I'm going to enjoy this trip to Vegas, thanks, Jinx."

"You're welcome! Why don't you go take a look around while I make some calls. We can get some food when I'm done. I'm starving."

"Yeah, I could eat."

"I got you, Paris."

I walked off to get a good look at the room. There were several huge flat screens in different areas all over the suite. It held a full kitchen and dining area, and the loft style living room was humongous and fully loaded with all the latest electronic gadgets. When I entered the bathroom, I wanted to strip down out of my clothes and soak in the huge spa tub. To say this room was beautiful would be an understatement.

"Jinx, I love this room. It's so spacious and cozy. I swear this is bringing back so many memories from my childhood. My dad was the best. He took me so many different places growing up."

"Your pops must've been that nigga." He grabbed my hand, leading me to the couch.

"My dad was definitely that nigga. I'm surprised you've never heard of him being that he was in the same type of business as you."

"What makes you say that, what type of business am I in?" he asked, grinning.

"I say that because I'm no fool. I see how you're living and your lifestyle. You didn't exactly get up and go to work this morning."

"What exactly are you saying, Paris?"

"I'm saying that I know what type of business you're into because my father was in the same business."

"Who is your father, Paris?" he asked with a face full of confusion.

"Have you ever heard of Adonis 'Don-Don' Monroe?"

"Wait a minute. Are you telling me the infamous Don-Don is your pops? No way!" He jumped up, getting hype.

"Yes, that's my father."

"I had you and your sister checked out the day you both stayed overnight at my house, but someone else was listed as your parents."

"My dad has always taken steps to ensure me and my sister were protected even in his absence. I'm positive he had something to do with that." I laughed at the thought.

"Growing up when I didn't know any better, I swear I wanted to be just like your pops. I didn't have a father. The stories I heard about The Don had me wanting to be his young protégé, but I don't fuck with cocaine or heroin."

"He wanted me to follow in his footsteps, but I had no interest in helping to run his empire."

"Your pops wanted you to be the heiress of his drug empire?"

"Yes, and I shut the thought down off top. Growing up the daughter of a kingpin, my life was like a movie some days— shootouts, fist fights, drug wars. You name it, and I've experienced it all. My father compensated my sister and me by taking us on shopping trips and lavish vacations for a lot of time he missed. I would have rather just spent time with my dad, you know."

"Yeah, I get it Paris, but my childhood was nothing like yours. I came from nothing, so I had to figure shit out on my own. Hustling and robbing niggas was my way out the hood. I had no father and my mama. Shit, I don't even want to talk about that bitch!"

"Why, Jinx? I'm a good listener."

"I don't want to talk about that. That's not why we're here."

"That's fine but remember nothing last forever, Jinx. You see what happened to my father."

"I've been doing this shit since I was a teenager."

"Start investing your money in different things. You have to clean your money up by opening up businesses. Why don't you give back to your community? There are so many different things you can do. You have the market on the east side and those dispensaries already so that's a start."

"I already got shit in motion P, don't trip."

"That's good to hear. You have a nice house, so that's a plus too."

"Enough about that, I already told you that's not why we're here. Come on, let's go get something to eat, Paris."

"I've been ready. I have a taste for seafood."

"I know the perfect spot on the strip."

We left the room walking hand in hand to the elevator. It felt like the natural thing to do, so I just went with the flow. It was a beautiful night in Vegas, and the weather was warm with a gentle breeze blowing, so we walked the short distance to the MB Steak located in the Hard Rock Hotel. By the time we arrived, it was after ten o'clock. The restaurant wasn't packed, and we were seated right away. Jinx requested a private room in the back of the restaurant away from everyone. After looking over the menu for a few minutes, we were ready to order. For dinner, we both ordered king crabs and filet mignon with cheesy mashed potatoes and broccoli on the side.

"Do you want to get something to drink, Paris?"

"Yes, I'll have some Hennessey and coke, and a lemon water please."

"I'll have the same, no lemon in my water tho. What I look like?" he laughed. After the waitress finished taking our order, we sat around having small talk until the food came out.

"Damn, these potatoes are good." Moaning, I put another spoonful in my mouth.

"All facts P, these cheesy potatoes fire. I got the munchies too, so I think I'ma need another round."

"Now you just being greedy." Taking my fork, I stole some food off his plate.

"Aye, what you doing woman?"

"I just wanted to see if your food was as good as mine."

"Yeah, whatever. How was your day before I picked you up?"

"My day was emotional. I had to bring the sheriff with me on a surprise home visit today, only to find a seven-year-old little girl at home with both parents who had died from a heroin overdose. It was the saddest thing to witness. The little girl said she had been trying to wake them up for two days. She told one of the officers that she thought they were both just tired."

"Damn, that's all bad. I feel for little mama. I know firsthand what she is going through."

"You still don't want to talk about it?"

"There ain't nothing to talk about." Jinx shrugged his shoulders while drinking his entire glass of Hennessy down in one gulp.

"Jinx, I don't know what you went through growing up, but it's ok to talk about the things that bother you. I can't force you to talk to me, but just know you can't heal from the things you keep buried inside of you. It just steals your peace."

"Paris, I swear to God I'ma marry you one day."

"What?" Laughing at his statement, I took a sip of my drink.

"You just spit some real shit, Paris. When I'm ready, I promise I will share that part of my life with you."

"Jinx, don't worry about that tonight. Do something for me."

"What is it?"

"Tonight while we're out on the strip, I want you to not worry about anything or anyone but you. Let's just live in the moment. I haven't done that shit in a long time."

"I'm wit it, Paris. I hope this shit don't get a nigga killed, but I'm down only for tonight."

"Cool, now let's get another drink Jinx."

Chapter Thirteen

JINX

Last night I had the best time I've ever had. I'm never able to just be free. I'm constantly looking over my shoulder on alert looking out for the ops. At dinner, Paris challenged me to just enjoy life. Me never being one to back down from a challenge, so I took her up on her offer. After dinner, for the rest of the night, we walked the strip talking about everything nothing being off limits. We stopped at different stores on the strip buying shit just because I could. We even went to a late night pirate show at Treasure Island. I would have never done no corny shit like that if I was in Vegas with my bros, but the show was cool. Afterwards we hit the casino gambling a little bit. Paris ended up winning ten thousand dollars at the crap table. Imagine her pretty ass being cold with the dice.

We ended our night around four o'clock this morning, drunk as fuck off Hennessey. I just knew she was gone let me fuck when we made it back to the room, but she went to take a shower then went straight to sleep on my ass. She did let me rub on her big booty all night till we both fell asleep though.

"Jinx, are you up?" Paris stretched, sitting up in the bed.

"I'm up. I've been sitting here thinking for the last hour."

"Oh yeah, what's on your mind?"

"Shit, just life, I have to make sure my next move is my best move, you feel me?"

"I hear you but just remember when it comes to this thing we call life you have to play chess, not checkers."

"You think you schooling me? I can tell you're the daughter of a kingpin," I teased.

"You swear you're a comedian. I told no lies though. What do you want to do today? I had a great time last night, thank you."

"What are you thanking me for, Paris?"

"For taking me on this getaway, I needed this. For the last few years, my focus has been on my family. Everything I do is for them, but last night you made everything about me, that hasn't happened in a long time, Jinx."

As she was talking, I don't know why, but I had the urge to kiss her fine ass. Even after a long night of drinking, she woke up looking good enough to eat.

"Why are you looking at me like that, Jinx?" She smiled nervously, fixing her hair that was all over the place.

"Have you ever fucked with a savage?"

"Once, he was my first love, and he meant a lot to me." Taking a deep breath then releasing it, Paris climbed out of bed walking into the bathroom. *Fuck!*

"You good, Paris?" I asked, walking up behind her as she brushed her teeth. I could see she wanted to cry when our eyes connected in the mirror. "What's wrong ma, talk to me?"

"I'm sorry, Jinx. You're good. Sometimes I just get emotional when I think about it."

"Who your ex?"

"Yes. It's just that you remind me so much of Quincy. Your entire vibe is just like his. Do you know he even complimented me calling me fine and pretty all the time, the same way you do? It's just creepy sometimes.

"We ain't the same tho, Paris."

"When you asked me if I ever fucked with a savage, my mind immediately went to him."

"I don't want to shit on the memories you and your ex have, but he and I are not the same niggas. I respect y'all history, and you're enti-tled to how you feel, Paris. I just want you to allow us to create our own memories together. You're with me now, ma."

She finished brushing her teeth then rinsed her mouth. When she was done, she turned to face me wrapping her arms around my neck while looking up at me.

"You got me feeling shit I shouldn't be feeling this soon, Jinx. Every time you come near me, my stomach is in knots."

Leaning down, I shut her up by covering her lips with mine. Pulling me closer, Paris deepened our kiss. When I heard her sexy ass moan-ing, a smile formed on my face. "What's so funny?"

"You are, Paris." Smirking, I backed away from her, stripped down out of my clothes, and then went to get in the shower. "Go get dressed P, we gotta get on the road soon," I called out from the shower.

"I'll be ready by the time you get out the shower. Oh yeah, and just for the record, we aren't together Jinx."

"Keep telling yourself that!" I laughed to myself.

After a relaxing shower, I walked out of the bathroom to find Paris sitting on the bed in nothing but a black lace thong. When she turned and noticed me standing there, she stood up covering her breasts with her hands walking over to her luggage, pulling out some jeans and a shirt.

"I thought you said you would be ready by the time I got out of the shower?" I questioned, walking up behind her with my towel wrapped around my waist.

"I'm sorry. I got on Facebook and got distracted. Give me five minutes, and I'll be ready." She smiled, turning around to face me. Walking up on her, I kissed her juicy lips.

"You know exactly what you doing walking around with this shit on."

"What's that?" She smiled, kissing me repeatedly on the lips.

"You see what you're doing to me? I'm not gone be able to control myself much longer if you don't put some clothes on," I warned, pushing my hard dick into her.

"Down boy." She laughed as she walked away with her clothes to the bathroom.

❧

We left Vegas headed back to LA because money called. I had to cut our trip short a day early, and I could tell that Paris was disappointed, but there would be other times. After a quick shopping spree at the mall on me, we hit the highway headed back to Los Angeles. There was traffic on Interstate 15, so it damn near took us 6 hours to get back to Cali. When I pulled in front of Paris' crib, I was surprised to see Gunna's car parked in the driveway.

"I wonder what my bro is doing over here?"

"Visiting my sister, I'm sure. I hope he doesn't break her heart. I think she really likes him."

"I didn't know they knew each other that well. Gunna has been through a lot, so your sister is gone have to have the patience to deal with his stubborn ass."

"I will try talking to her, but yeah, they were really good friends at one point. They went to school together for a while, I guess."

"Gunna is stubborn, but he's solid, so don't worry."

"You want to come in and maybe watch a movie before you have to leave?"

"Yeah, I can come in for an hour or so, but then I have to go handle some business."

"I get it, no need to explain."

"Let me get your bags. Go unlock the door. I'm right behind you."

When we got to the front door, it was slightly open.

"Step back, Paris, let me go in first." I walked in the door with my pistol locked and loaded. I took a quick look around the room, and nothing seemed out of place.

"I hear noises coming from the kitchen," Paris whispered. We slowly crept around the corner into the kitchen. "LUNDYN!" Paris screamed, burying her face into my arm to shield her eyes.

"Ooh shit, Gunna, eat this pussy baby! Umm hmm yes, shit this feels so good!" I cried out in pleasure as Gunna circled his tongue over my clit rapidly.

After tonight there was no way that I was ever leaving his fine ass alone, not after experiencing this award worthy head. I'm ready to wife this nigga up. I'm laying here with my mind gone, eyes rolling in the back of my head, thinking about what our future kids will look like. Gunna was about to have me sleeping outside of his bedroom window at night singing "Dangerously In Love" to him.

"Oh shit Gunna just like that! Yesss eat it, baby! Oooh shit, I'm about to cum!"

"Oh my god, LUNDYN!" I heard my sister screaming, but I was in a zone so far away that I didn't want to come back to reality no time soon.

"Cum one more time for me, ma!" Gunna mumbled, lapping up my juices with his long tongue.

The way my body was reacting to him had me drooling at the mouth. I couldn't even focus on my sister walking in on me. Hell, she wasn't supposed to be back till tomorrow. Gunna had me laid back on the island in the middle of the kitchen with my legs pushed back as far behind my head as they could stretch, kneeling and eating my kitty like it would be his last meal.

"Oh shit, I'm cumming!" I screamed, trying to push his head away with my hands, but he wouldn't let up. After feasting on my goodies a few more seconds, Gunna finally pulled his face from in between my legs, wiping his mouth with the back of his hand.

"What's good bro, sup fish lips?" Gunna turned, acknowledging both Paris and Jinx presence. He then quickly put his attention back on me. "Which way is your bedroom? I'm not done with you yet, ma. That pussy is sweet as a muthafucka!" I hungrily kissed his lips, tasting my own juices.

"It's around this corner to the end of the hall on the right," I panted, breathlessly pulling away from Gunna.

Jinx cleared his throat, trying to get our attention. I buried my face into Gunna's chest in shame when it finally registered in my brain that Jinx was standing next to my sister,

"You nasty little bitch! I can't believe you in here fuckin' in the kitchen of all places, Lundyn!" Paris screamed, burying her head in Jinx's arm.

I didn't mind my sister seeing me damn near naked, but Jinx seeing me in this predicament was a different story.

"Sorry Paris, I didn't know you were on the way home," I called out to her as Gunna carried me out of the kitchen bridal style. When we made it to my bedroom, he closed the door with his foot. "Put me down."

Carrying me over to my bed, he dropped me down on my soft pillow top mattress, pulling me to the center of the bed by my feet. My heart was beating out of my chest anticipating his next move. It was so quiet that I could hear my heart beating.

"Don't get scared now, Lun." Smirking, he climbed on top of me. When our eyes locked, goosebumps covered my entire body as chills ran up and down my spine.

"You pretty as fuck, Lundyn."

"Thank you." Blushing, I pulled him down closer to me.

"You know that I should have killed that nigga Rasheed tonight behind yo ass, right?"

"You were wrong, Gunna. Things should have never gone that far."

"You disrespected me."

"I did not! I told you I was dating. How was I to know we would run into Rasheed at the movies tonight?" I moaned as he planted soft kisses all over my warm skin. My body shuddered from his touch. "Damn, this feels so good, Gunna." He looked up staring intensely into my eyes, giving me butterflies.

"I don't want you fuckin' with no other niggas, Lundyn," he randomly blurted out, catching me off guard. "Fuck that nigga Rasheed or whatever the fuck you said his name was. He's lucky I didn't kill him like I wanted to ona gang!"

"What?" I asked, sitting up, pushing him off me.

"You heard me, Lundyn. If I hear about you fucking with another nigga besides me from this day forward, I'ma kill you and that nigga."

"Now you're doing too much, don't you think?"

"Did you hear what the fuck I just said? Play with me and see what happens."

"You don't own me, Gunna."

"I do now. You belong to me. I don't go around eating just any female's pussy. Matter of fact, this pussy belongs to me now too! You're definitely my bitch, fuck what you talking about," Laughing, he went back to kissing me like he didn't just snap at me.

"Nigga you're 51/50."

"Take this shit off! We've done enough talking," he instructed, standing up removing his clothes from his tall frame.

His light skin was painted with colorful tattoos. I stared at the savage life tattoo covering his back, thinking it must've hurt. When he reached into his pants pocket, pulling out a Magnum XL condom, I was able to get a better look at his tattoo. I could tell it was covering up several scars.

Tearing the magnum open with his teeth, he tossed the wrapper to the floor. I wanted to ask him about the scars on his back, but decided against it, saying the first thing that came to mind instead.

"That tattoo on your back is dope."

"Good lookin' out, this shit is old as fuck." I couldn't believe my eyes, as I watched him roll the condom onto his long, thick dick.

Crawling over to the edge of the bed where he was standing, I stood on my feet getting eye level with him. We kissed after staring at each other for a brief moment.

"Let me get on top, Gunna?" I asked while stroking his erection in my hands.

"You better ride this muthafucka properly, or don't even waste my time, Lun," he smirked, picking me up. I wrapped my legs around his waist, arms around his neck, just as he lifted my body, slowly sliding me down on his pole.

"Sssssssssss oh my god, Gunna!" I whimpered, as he filled me up completely.

"Fuckkkkkk!" he groaned, biting down on my bottom lip, while I bounced up and down finding my rhythm. "Aye, yo pussy is good as fuck, Lundyn. This shit is tight and dumb wet," he uttered in disbelief.

"Fuck me, Gunna!" I cried from the pleasure and pain that I was experiencing.

"I'm finna murder this little pussy!" he mumbled, carrying me over to the opposite side of my bedroom where there was more space.

After making sure I was secure in his arms, he began stroking me again while moving his body up and down as if he was doing squats. I had never been in this position before, so I was clawing at his back because of how deep he was inside of me. I had tears in my eyes threatening to fall from feeling as if I was being ripped in half.

"Oh my god, yessss!"

He hit my spot repeatedly, fucking me with precision while I grinded my hips as best as I could.

"Yesssss, Gunna! Fuck meeeee! Yess, ummm shit!"

"You gone stop fucking with other niggas?" he asked while slamming into me full force. I completely ignored his crazy ass while we matched each other stroke for stroke. "Fuck! This little pussy got some power!"

Right when I was getting ready to cum, he picked me up, flipping me upside down like I weighed nothing.

"Cancel all them niggas you been texting!" he demanded, taking my swollen clit into his mouth.

I ignored him removing the condom covering his dick. My mouth watered from the anticipation of pleasing him. After stroking him a few times in my hands, I hungrily took him into my mouth. Quickly I caught a steady rhythm while licking and slurping around the head like it was a lollipop.

"That's right. Get all that dick, Lun!" *Smack!*

Obeying his orders, I took him inch by inch into the back of my mouth, not stopping until I damn near gagged.

Smack!

"Lundyn, I said get all of my dick!" I deep throated the rest of him until it disappeared in my mouth. "Get my nuts too ma, fuck!" he demanded going back and forth between sucking my clit and licking my ass. *Smack! Smack!*

Oh, this nigga eats ass too, I'm definitely not leaving Gunna alone. I thought to myself.

"I'm about to cummmmm Gunna, shitttt!"

"Shit awww fuck, me tooo!" he hollered out just as I started cumming. He was smacking my ass over and over again while slurping on my clit. I knew he was getting ready to cum, so I opened my mouth wide, allowing him to release his seeds in my mouth. I made sure to catch every last drop. Gunna was out of breath, heavily panting trying to catch his breath by the time I finished draining him.

"Yeah, you most definitely better not be out here fucking and sucking no other nigga, the way you just fucked me," Gunna warned me while flipping me back around on my feet.

"Damn, Gunna, that shit was fire!"

"Yessiiirrr!" He laughed, pulling my naked body close to his.

"How did we go from arguing at the movies, to you damn near killing Rasheed, to us fucking and sucking each other like porn stars?"

"It doesn't even matter how it happened, Lundyn. I'm just glad it did. I'm not letting you go ever again."

"Boy please, that was just sex. You don't have to say that just to make me feel special."

"Stop fuckin' playing with me, Lundyn!"

"I'm not playing. Until you can show me I'm the only female you checkin' for, I'm going to continue doing whatever my single ass heart desires," I smirked, walking into the bathroom to handle my hygiene.

While I stood at the bathroom sink brushing my teeth, Gunna walked up behind me. We stood staring at each other in the mirror, no words being exchanged. After a brief staring match, he wrapped his arms around my waist while kissing his way down my neck. Looking at him through the mirror, I bit down on my bottom lip, releasing a soft moan, loving the way he was making my body feel. After a few more minutes of us lusting over one another, I finished brushing my teeth.

"You really want me to act crazy over your pretty ass, don't you?"

"No, I'm just not about to be out here playing myself. I've heard all about how you and the Savage Boyz get down."

"You ain't ever heard my name in the streets connected with no bitch! If a female's out here saying I'm her nigga, she's a fucking lie!"

"Why you getting so hyped up, Gunna?" I asked, turning around to face him."

"I want you, Lundyn."

"It's funny how good pussy will have a nigga changing his tune."

"I've been feeling this way about you, Lundyn. It has nothing to do with us just having sex. I know I fucked up in the past playing games and not being real with you about how I felt, but right now, I'm dead ass serious, you belong to me."

"Yeah ok, boo."

"Lundyn, my bitch ain't about to be out here fucking with no other niggas."

I walked away from him with a satisfied smile on my face totally ignoring what he was talking about. *How the tables have turned.* There was no way I was gonna just cut off all communication with my boos after one night of good sex. I don't care how good the dick is.

The Next Morning

"Lundyn, I know we just started kicking it again, but I feel like we can be together on some real lovey-dovey type shit," Gunna expressed while he ran his fingers through my hair massaging my scalp.

"Gunna, believe it or not, I waited so long to hear these words from you. So please don't get me wrong. I like you, but we just linked back up. I want us to take things slow. I know we been fuckin' all night, and honestly, I don't regret anything about being intimate with you. All I'm saying is let's reconnect, you know get to know each other all over before you start claiming me as yours."

"I hear what you saying, but I go after what I want. Right now, I want you."

"Well let's see if you feel the same way next week. I can be a lot to deal with at times."

"I ain't worried about what you talking bout. Besides, I'm always up for the challenge."

"Remember, you said that."

"Aye, the S Boyz have a kickback coming up next weekend. Why don't you come out and chill with me?"

"I have to see what my sister wants to do first. I think we were going to visit our dad, so I can't make you any promises."

"Just let me know if you can make it, your sister can come too. I'm sure my brother Jinx would be cool with it. I think he's feeling yo sister big lip ass anyway." He laughed.

"What I tell you about talking about my sister's lips?"

"It's just jokes, calm yo ass down. I'll talk about your big head ass too."

"Yeah, whatever, punk." I sat up stretching before getting out of bed.

"Where you going?"

"To help you find your clothes so that I can walk you out."

"Ain't this about a bitch. You gone get the dick then put a nigga out afterwards. I feel used." He laughed, shaking his head.

"No silly it's just time for you to go boo."

"You lucky I got business to handle this morning."

"Text me later. You got the number." He put his clothes and shoes on then headed for the door. "Let me walk you outside."

"Yeah, you do that but put something else on first." Not wanting to argue, I got my bathrobe hanging behind the door then put it on. "Now, you can walk me out."

"Let's go."

Walking the short distance to his car parked in the driveway, he hit

the alarm to unlock his door, then cut the car on. Stepping back
outside the car, he grabbed me, pulling me close to him.

"I want you to think about coming to the kickback, alright?"

"I'll talk to my sister. Text me later, and I'll let you know."

"Ok, I'll do just that." He stared at me for a moment then kissed
my lips. "Let me get my ass up out of here before I get carried away. I'll
text you later. I got business to handle, and I need to go home to
shower and shit first."

"Talk to you later Gunna, that was way too much information." I
smiled as he went to get back inside of his car. I waited in the driveway
watching him until he hit the corner, and then I went back inside to
shower.

Chapter Fifteen

PARIS

Waking up this morning, I looked over to my left at my empty bed. Memories from the night before started slowly running through my mind. Jinx and I drank almost a fifth of Hennessy together last night after things settled down. I was devastated walking in on my sister in the kitchen last night. I knew she was having sex, but I never wanted to catch her in the act. After the initial shock wore off, I was able to enjoy the rest of my time with Jinx. We talked for hours while drinking Hennessy until two in the morning eventually falling asleep together. I was surprised he stayed as long as he did because he said he had business to handle, but I'm glad he did.

Pulling the covers off my body, I got out of bed walking into the bathroom to do my normal morning routine. As I was washing my face, I looked down, and there was a note on the bathroom counter with my name on it. Next to the note were stacks of hundred-dollar bills. The note read:

Paris,

Good morning, beautiful. I didn't want to wake you when I left early this morning because you looked so peaceful. I enjoyed your company again last night. It turns out you're not so boring after all. Hahaha! You just need to get out of the house more and live a little. Let your sister live her life. She's grown. Stop worrying about your family to the point that you forget about taking time for yourself. They will be straight, regardless. Take this money I'm leaving you. Go out today and get your hair and nails done. Buy yourself some sexy shit to wear and then call me if you want to link up. Maybe we can go to dinner or the movies. If not, I still want you to do something for yourself. Since you're always focused on everyone else's needs before your own, I want you to put yourself first today ma. Hit me! (323)337-7309

-Jinx

After reading his note once more, I stared at myself in the mirror smiling from ear to ear. Jinx was most definitely rough around the edges, but underneath all his rough exterior was a good person. At first, I was a little skeptical about us spending so much time together so soon, but I'm glad I made the decision to just go with the flow of things.

"Good morning, sissy poo." Lundyn smiled, calling me by the pet name she gave me when she was a little girl.

"I should fuck you up! Sissy poo my ass, bitch!" I snapped, walking back into my bedroom. Lundyn's hot pussy ass was lying across my bed with a huge smile on her face.

"Paris, I'm so sorry. I didn't mean for you to walk in and catch me in the kitchen like that. I don't even know how it happened. One minute we were arguing about him tripping on Rasheed, then the next he had me in the kitchen grinding my pussy in his face."

"Wait, he got into it with your little boo Rasheed?"

"Yes, and it got ugly real quick sis. I've never been so embarrassed in my life." She laughed, shaking her head.

Gunna has absolutely no chill, whatsoever. He didn't care about witnesses or being in a public place. All he knew was he felt disrespected by Rasheed approaching me while we were together."

"Well sis, that had to be a little awkward, don't you think?"

"Yeah, but Gunna acted like we're married and he walked in on me fucking Rasheed behind his back. Then Rasheed's goofy ass made the situation worse by telling him how good my pussy tasted, and how I would always come back to him."

"That's why that nigga was eating that kitty like it was the last supper?" I laughed so hard that I had tears in my eyes.

"You were looking like you were having an out-of-body experience, sister. If you could've seen how you were looking at him before he carried you out the kitchen." I continued laughing. "Lun, it's obvious your mind is gone boo. You're clearly in love with that rude ass nigga."

"Was it that obvious?" She laughed, clutching her imaginary pearls. "I've missed him so much. I really wish we would've hooked up sooner."

"Just be careful with him. I know you don't want me in your personal business. However, I can't help but worry about you. You're my little sister, so I'm always going to feel like I have to protect you. I would never want you to go through what I went through when I lost Quincy. That shit devastated me and left me in a deep depression for months before I was able to function properly. I still have days where I'm barely able to get out of bed because of nightmares that torment me."

"I know, Paris. What happened to Quincy was fucked up, but over time, you got through it. Most importantly, we got through it together."

"Enough about Quincy, tell me what happened after y'all left the kitchen last night?" I inquired being nosey.

"Magic, sis." She smiled, staring off into space. "That's the only way I can describe it."

"Damn, it was that good?"

"Magical Paris, the sex was so good that afterwards he was telling me I can't talk to no one else but him."

"Yeah, your night must've been really magical," I teased. "What time did he leave?"

"He just left not too long ago. I went to shower, then came to see what you were up to. How was your getaway with Jinx, and where did y'all go?"

"We went to Las Vegas, and I can't lie. I had a really good time. During the car ride, I was able to clear my head and get some good sleep. Jinx is dope all the way around, Lundyn."

"Vegas! He took you to Las Vegas?"

"Yes sis, we stayed at the Bellagio Hotel in a presidential suite."

"Damn, I'm jealous. What did you bring me back? I know you got me something. Where is it at?"

"It's in my bag downstairs. I have to get it. I won ten thousand dollars too."

"Doing what?"

"At the crap table. You know Quincy taught me how to shoot dice in high school. The crap table is really not that different. I turned one hundred-dollars into ten thousand in less than an hour."

"Girl you sound like one of them scammers on Instagram." She fell over on the bed laughing uncontrollably.

"Get your crazy ass out of my room so that I can get dressed. I ain't no damn scammer." I laughed, walking into my closet.

"Where you going?"

"Jinx left me some money to go shopping with, but I can shop anytime. I got a call from dad not too long ago. He didn't sound like himself, so I'm going to go visit him today since it's still early."

"Let me go get dressed. I'm going with you."

"No, I have to take this drive by myself today. There are some things I need to discuss with him."

"What are you not telling me?"

"I'll talk to you more about it later, Lundyn. I have to get dressed."

Later That Day

I was all in my feelings driving away from the Federal Correctional Institution in Victorville, California. Every time I went to visit my father, it was hard for me because I hated to see him locked up like an animal. It's been years, and I still can't get used to seeing him in prison. My pops is a hood legend, a self-made boss in his own right. In my eyes, he was my very own personal superhero. Whenever he walked into a room, his presence was felt. Everyone knew Adonis 'The Don' Monroe wasn't the nigga to fuck with. However, I was caught off guard when I saw him today. He was on edge, and he looked tired, highly stressed, and worn out. His appearance had changed drastically in just a month. He even lost about twenty pounds, which was a clear sign something was going on with him.

The visit started good. He came out, we hugged, then sat down across from each other. We made small talk, catching up as we always did. After talking for less than ten minutes, he switched gears and jumped straight into the bullshit. Our conversation went left real fast, further letting me know something was off with my dad.

"Princess, since you're here, we might as well discuss the reason I asked you to come see me."

"What is it, dad? I'm listening."

"You know I've done a lot for this family over the years, and when I came to prison, I lost everything I worked hard for."

"I know dad, that's why I make sure your commissary stays stacked, and you get everything you ask me for. I appreciate everything you did for our family growing up."

"That's good to hear because I need a huge favor from you."

"Ok, just tell me what it is." He leaned in, checking his surroundings to make sure no one was paying us any attention before he started talking.

"In a few days, I'm going to text you an address. Go to the address, then ask for Pablo San Andreas Sr. Let him know the Don sent you to make good on that favor he owes me."

"Wait, I'm confused, dad. What favor does he owe you? I need to know what I'm walking into."

"Let me finish, and I'll get to that part."

"Just spill it, dad. Stop wasting my time dancing around the topic." I sighed, sensing this was something I more than likely didn't want to do.

"Pablo is going to give you five kilos of cocaine," he explained barely above a whisper.

"Have you lost your mind?" I snapped through clenched teeth.

"Listen, Paris Monroe! I am your father, and you will do as I say! Now, I need you to put a team together and move this product for me just like I taught you when you were younger. I will be home soon. Then I will take over, and you can go back to your little social worker job." He laughed, however, I didn't find shit funny.

"You must have fallen and bumped your head! If you think I'm about to stop my life to fulfill your little kingpin fantasy, you're wrong!"

"Excuse me?"

"You heard what I said! I'm not doing it, period! I have spent the last few years degrading myself for money while going to school and working my ass off to get to where I am. That is not about to change for you or anyone else."

"You will do what I asked, and that's final!"

"You and Pablo can kiss my ass!"

"You disloyal bitch! I gave you everything, and this is how you do me? You never wanted for anything growing up! You had your first designer bag before you were a month old!"

"That has nothing to do with what you're asking me to do! This is my life, not yours!"

"Oh, I guess because you stop shaking your ass down at that booty club like a fuckin' slut, you think you're too good, huh? Is that what it is?"

"Fuck you, dad! I don't know what has gotten into you, but I want nothing to do with the new you!"

"Leave and don't come back, bitch!" he snapped, jumping up out of his seat, knocking it over. *"Until you change your mind you are dead to me, Paris!"*

"Wh- What?" I asked, stumbling over my words.

"You heard me! I'm ashamed you are a part of my bloodline. You're a disgrace to the Monroe name. It doesn't matter how many degrees you have or what you did for me these last few years. You will always be remembered as a stripper hoe!"

He laughed and then spat in my direction before flipping over the table that separated us. The guards rushed over in a hurry wrestling my dad to the ground. I was in disbelief watching my father show his ass.

"Fuck you, dad, how dare you talk to me this way!"

"Get the fuck out bitch and don't come back! You are dead to me! Until you do what I asked, you are no longer my daughter!"

Fresh tears freely ran down my face snapping me out of my thoughts. Today's events kept replaying in my mind, and my feelings were hurt. I always thought my dad respected and loved me just the same, in spite of his disappointment in my decision not to be a part of his drug empire when I was a teenager. However, I was wrong. He showed me his true colors today, and it fucked me up inside. I under-stand my dad lost everything when he went to prison. That still doesn't give him the right to expect me to pick up the pieces when I've done more than enough.

I still have no interest in being a dope girl. I didn't want that life for myself. It never has been something I wanted to do. I have no issue if that's how you choose to get your bag. I salute you, but it's not my thing. My dad throwing the fact that I danced in my face hurt me the most because I was doing that to provide for my family and pay for school. Not saying my past choices were the best, but luckily, everything worked out for me in the end.

After all the disrespect, he had the nerve to ask me to leave, refusing the rest of our visit. My heart ripped in half watching him being dragged out of the visiting room. Hearing him yell that I was dead to him and not to return until I changed my mind nearly brought me to my knees. How could he be so cruel knowing how far I drove to see him? He has obviously lost his mind. Not once did he stop to ask himself why I didn't want to get involved in the same fucked up shit that took him and my mother away from me. Instead, he insulted me in the worst way. The words he spoke felt like a knife was plunged deep into my chest.

When my parents are released from prison, they will have missed out on years they could have been spending enjoying life and traveling the world together. One thing I learned from my parents' incarceration was that it doesn't matter how much you think you know the dope game or how far your reach is, eventually the lifestyle will catch up with you.

My emotions were all over the place as I drove the freeway back home. I knew Lundyn was probably out running the streets since it was the weekend, so I didn't even bother to call her with my drama. I hadn't talked to my bestie Dream in a few days, so I called her up.

Ring! Ring!

"Well, well, well, if it isn't my long lost best friend. Why haven't I heard from you since last week? I know you got my text last night, bitch!" Dream spat with an attitude.

"Don't act like you haven't been out of town friend."

"Chris flew me out to Jamaica for a few days. I told you I would be gone, didn't I?"

"Yes, you told me."

"That still doesn't give you the right to ignore my calls, Paris."

"I was out with my new lil boo last night. That's why I didn't answer."

"Girl, stop it. You're not trying to mess with nobody but that dildo you probably done worn the rubber off of."

"Fuck you, Dream." I laughed happy that she was putting me in a better mood. "I'm serious though, friend. I just got back from Las Vegas last night."

"Who is he? I need details, bitch."

"I'm not telling you shit unless you come to my house and have a drink with me. I've had a shitty day."

"Are you cooking?"

"Yes, I have a taste for enchiladas."

"I'm sold. When I get there, you had better have me a margarita waiting along with this tea. It better be good and juicy too, boo."

"Bye Dream, I'll be home in about two hours. I'm on the way home from visiting my dad."

"Oh yeah, how is he doing?"

"Girl a whole ass mess, but I'll tell you about his ass later."

"Alright Paris, I'll call you when I'm on the way. See you later, boo."

"Bye, friend."

🍃

Two hours later, I was back in the city and leaving Food 4 Less in Gardena. As I drove down Artesia Boulevard, my phone started ringing. Jinx popped up on the caller ID, and butterflies came to my stomach. I loved the attention he gave me as well as the effort he put into getting to know me. It was so refreshing.

"Hello."

"What's up, Paris? Where you at?"

"On my way home, I need a drink. My day was terrible," I whined into the phone.

"What happened, Paris? Did you not go shopping with the money I left for you?"

"No, I chose to go see my dad instead. I can shop anytime. Thanks for the money though. That was the sweetest thing anyone has done for me in such a long time."

"You're welcome. How was the visit? I know pops was happy to see you."

"The visit was horrible. I drove an hour and a half, all the way to Victorville, and we got into a huge argument. He acted such a fool that he was dragged out of the visiting room by the prison guards." I sighed into the phone."

"Damn ma, that's wild as fuck."

"Right, that's why I need a drink. My best friend is supposed to be stopping by in about an hour. Maybe I'll feel better after I have some Patrón in my system."

"What y'all about to do?"

"Nothing really, we'll probably have a few drinks and talk some shit while I cook dinner. I told you I had a bad day."

"Let me help make the rest of your day better. I could use a drink. Pull up on me."

"Not today, Jinx. All I want to do is unwind and sip on some Patrón with my hair all over my head looking nice and ugly." I laughed, trying to lighten the mood.

"Listen ma. I'm on the east side on 98th and Main Street. Call me when you hit the block so that I can come outside."

"Wait! I never said I was coming, Jinx."

"You seem like you could use my company, and I could eat. Since your about to cook, it only makes sense for us to be together. We can help each other out, you feel me?"

"Where is your car? I don't feel like driving way over to the east side right now, Jinx."

"Man, Gunna picked me up this morning because we had business to handle together. As soon as your sister called him, that nigga left me on the block to go pick her up with his ole lovesick ass. I have never seen him act this way over any female."

"Hahaha! Leave him alone, Jinx. Gunna is an asshole, but I think the feelings between them are mutual. I'm just worried they're moving a little too fast. They just reconnected a couple of weeks ago under crazy circumstances, so they need to take things slow."

"You're always worrying about something. You need to learn how to relax and let shit happen the way it's supposed to. I'll see you when you get here. Pull up!" *Click!*

This nigga hung up on me. Lord knows I wasn't in the mood for his shenanigans, but I guess a little company wouldn't be so bad. I could use a booty rub. I made a U-turn in the middle of the street then drove down to Vermont Avenue to get on the 110 freeway.

During the short drive to the east side, I couldn't keep my mind off the situation with my dad. In twenty-five years, I couldn't remember a time my dad was mad at me. Although I was hurt by his actions today, I was going to stand firm in my decision. If that meant my dad was gone say fuck me because of it, then fuck him too—period!

Fifteen minutes later, I was on the east side of Los Angeles rolling down Main Street. When I turned on 98th Street, the block was packed with cars parked right in the middle of the street. Niggas were posted up smoking weed and playing loud music from their car stereos. My phone rang, so I slowed down to see if I saw Jinx in the crowd. I didn't see him, so I stopped the car to answer the phone.

"Hello."

"Aye, pull up in front of the white house in the middle of the block. I see you. You're about four houses down from me."

"You mean the white house next to where all them niggas are hanging outside at?"

"Yeah, that ain't nobody but my peoples. They doing a whole lot of gang shit, but don't trip they know you with me."

"Ok, I'm here now so come outside. There is food in the trunk, and I don't want it to go bad."

"I'm on my way."

Click!

All eyes were on me as I sat in my G-Wagon parked in the middle of the street.

Bam! Bam! Bam! I jumped back startled by a handsome brown-skinned guy covered in tattoos banging on my window.

"Quit banging on my damn window! What the fuck is your problem?" I snapped with an attitude.

"Roll the window down, my bad, beautiful." I sighed, rolling my window down halfway to see what this fool wanted.

"What's up?" I asked just as Jinx opened the passenger side door sliding into the seat.

"Aye, you ain't got no homegirls you can hook me up with that's pretty like you?"

"Ummm, no!" I laughed in his face. I hated me a *hook me up with your friend* ass nigga. That shit was so annoying to me.

"Black, get yo ass on bro." Jinx laughed, brushing him off.

"Be nice, Jinx," I suggested, trying to lighten the mood. "Seriously though, I don't have no friends. Well, I have one friend, but she's not going to be interested. Trust me."

"Hook a nigga up. The ladies love me?"

"Paris, pull off." Jinx chuckled while reclining the seat back. "Hit me later on, Black," Jinx added, pulling a blunt from behind his ear. All I could do was shake my head as I pulled off, leaving him standing there. "Get on the 110 freeway."

"Why? I was going to take the streets to my house."

"Let's just go to my house in San Pedro. You can cook and have drinks over there."

"I need to be comfortable when I cook Jinx."

"I got some shit at the house you can wear just go."

"I can't. I have work first thing in the morning."

"Whatever just drive, shit."

"I've had a rough day. Don't be rude. I can always drop you back off where you were and then take my ass home alone! I'm going to my house because I can't miss work. Tomorrow I have a full day."

"Man, be quiet and just go to your house, you big baby." He laughed, grabbing my hand and kissing my fingers one by one. "Is it cool if I invite my bro over to keep your friend company?"

"I don't know, Jinx. My bestie is stuck up. I don't want her being rude to your brother."

"I'm not worried about that. He's cool people. Just don't act weird when he gets there."

"Oh Lord, now I'm nervous."

"Don't be, can I spark this blunt up?"

"Yeah, just let me turn on the air conditioner first."

"This G-Wagon rides smooth as fuck. If I weren't into Chevy's, I would get me one."

"Thank you. I love my car. I want to get it wrapped and put some rims on it, but I haven't had a chance to do it yet."

When we made it to my house, Jinx grabbed the bags for me out of the trunk and then carried them inside.

"Jinx, please put everything in the kitchen while I go change out of these clothes. Make yourself comfortable. There is plenty of snacks in there if you want something to hold you over till the food is ready."

"Alright cool."

The first thing I did when I entered my bedroom was let my hair down and strip out of my clothes. I had a cute black lace maxi dress lying on my bed, so I put that on with my new Chanel slides Jinx bought me while we were in Vegas. I added my favorite Sephora lip gloss to my lips and then made my way back downstairs. Jinx crept up behind me, scaring the shit out of me when I entered the kitchen.

"Please don't scare me like that, Jinx!" I screamed, holding my chest.

"My bad ma, I just came from outside looking at the backyard. We gone have to get up in that pool together."

"What are you doing roaming all over my house, punk?"

"Shit, you said to get comfortable, so that's what I did." He shrugged, walking me backwards into the refrigerator. "Your house is nice. I might need you to come redecorate my crib," He smiled, staring down at me, pushing my hair back out of my face.

"Thanks, but I meant to get comfortable as in taking your shoes off and maybe watch some TV while I cook," I teased, staring into his beautiful brown eyes. Jinx had my stomach twisted in knots antici-pating his next move. "Why are you looking at me like that?"

"No reason, I'm just looking at your lips. They are just as soft as them big muthafuckas look," he teased, making me blush.

Jinx has never really made any type of moves on me other than kissing here and there. We flirted, but that's about it, so his sudden display of affection surprised me. Standing on my toes, I pressed my lips up against his kissing him softly.

"Are they still soft enough for you?" I asked with a huge grin on my face.

"I really couldn't tell. I need another kiss, and then I'll let you know wit yo fine ass."

Standing on my toes once again, I kissed him, but this time I got nasty with it and added a little tongue. My nipples hardened, and my clit began to throb aching to be touched. In the heat of the moment, I pulled back panting, trying to catch my breath.

"Damn Paris, you doing it like that ma?" He smiled, adjusting his hard-on. "You got my dick tryna break free."

"You're so nasty." I laughed, playfully hitting his arm.

"Shit, I'm serious. We both grown. I'm telling the truth. My dick is hard as fuck." Taking my hand, he placed it on his erection.

"Let me see it?" I asked, feeling bold.

"Pull it out," he challenged, kissing my lips. He was wearing a Jordan jogger set, so I had easy access. When I stuck my hand inside of his pants, I gasped surprised by the size of him.

"That muthafucka beautiful ain't it, Paris?" He smirked.

"Damn Jinx, you are walking around with a weapon of mass destruction! This is too much dick for one person," I mumbled with wide eyes, fanning my face with my hand. My body got hot as I felt my juices start to flow.

"You funny as fuck, Paris." He laughed, putting his dick back in his pants. "You will learn to adjust. When I put this dick in yo life, you gone be begging me to beat that pussy up!"

"That thing won't be going anywhere near me."

"I bet that pussy's wet as fuck right now."

"You swear that you know everything."

"So, I'm lying?"

"Yep," I lied with a straight face.

"Let me see, then?"

"No nasty," I nervously laughed, trying to walk away.

"Nah fuck that, let me see. I know yo ass lying to me right now." He grabbed me, kissing me on the lips.

"If I'm lying, then what?" I mumbled in between kisses.

"If you lying, then you gotta let me make that pussy cum."

"Move nasty," I pushed back, breaking away from him and walked over to the counter to remove the items from inside the bags.

"You scary as fuck, P."

"No, I'm not Jinx. I'm just not about to let you split me wide open."

"I don't need to use my dick to make you cum, Paris," he smirked, walking up on me. "A nigga just wants to please you. I know that pussy wet. If I'm wrong, prove it to me."

"You make it so hard to resist you, Jinx," I confessed.

"Is it wet?" I nodded my head up and down. "Can I see how wet yo pussy is?" I nodded my head up and down again, giving him permission.

"Can I tell you something Jinx, promise not to laugh?"

"Yeah what's up, ma?"

"I'm scared. The last time I felt like this, I ended up heartbroken. Losing my ex almost broke me mentally. I can't ever go back to that dark place."

"Don't be scared, Paris," I gasped as Jinx raised my dress, pulling my thong to the side, slowly pushing his middle finger inside if me. "Let's create our own memories, P. Your ex and I are not the same niggas. I need you to remember that, baby."

"Ahhh!" I cried out, throwing my head back as he added another finger inside of me while circling my clit with his thumb.

"You like that shit?" I couldn't speak, so I nodded my head up and down saying yes.

"I want to hear you say that shit, answer me!" he hissed, biting down on my neck while sucking the skin lightly.

"Yes, Jinx, I love it. It feels so good."

"What feels good?" he uttered in a low tone, circling my clit at a rapid pace.

"Sssssshit!"

"What's wrong ma, talk to me?" he voiced, giving me a look that I couldn't read. "Answer me!"

"Jinx, please don't stop. I'm about to cum!"

"Where you want to cum at?"

"What?"

"You want to come on my fingers, or in my mouth, Paris?" he asked, trailing light kisses along my neck, at the same time stroking my pussy so good that I was on the verge of losing my mind.

"Let me cum on your dick, Jinx!" I moaned out loud, saying the first thing that came to mind.

"You not ready for that yet." Removing his hand from my wetness, he licked my juices off his fingers one by one. "Your pussy is sweet just like I knew it would be."

"I was about to cum. Why did you stop?" He picked me up and carried me over to the table in the dining room.

"I got you, Paris. Lay back and let me take care of this pussy."

"Jinx no, please put it in. That can wait."

"You not ready for the dick."

"I am, Jinx." I scooted to the edge of the table and pulled his dick out of his boxers, lining it up with my opening.

"Fuck is you doing, Paris?" he moaned while I smacked my clit with his pole, playing in my wetness. "You just gone take what you want, huh?" he smirked, biting down on his bottom lip. "What happened to you saying I wasn't putting my dick nowhere near you?"

"Put it in Jinx!" I snapped feeling like I was about to lose it.

"Oh you begging for the dick," he mumbled, sliding the tip slowly inside of me. "Fuck, P!" he groaned, tossing his head back. "Open up for me, baby!" He pulled back, leaning down and circling my clit with his long tongue.

"Ah shit, yessss!"

"Umm-hmm, talk to me!"

"Eat it, baby, yessssss!" I could feel my orgasm approaching just that fast. Using my hand, I gripped the back of his head, locking him in place. "Do that shit, daddy, don't stop!"

"Umm-hmm that's what I like to hear. Cum for me," he mumbled, lapping his tongue over my clit rapidly. "Look at me, Paris!"

Starting from my toes, my body began to tremble. Right when my orgasm hit me, Jinx pulled back slamming his dick into me damn near splitting me in half.

"Ahhh yesss, I'm cumming!"

Ding Dong!

"That's your doorbell?"

"Fuck me, Jinx, that door can wait!" He did just that. His stroke game was vicious, and he didn't miss a beat as he pounded my insides.

"Cum again so you can get the door."

"Let me up." He pulled out of me, holding his dick in his hand. Turning around, I bent over holding on to the counter, tooting my ass up in the air. "Come teach me about that savage life."

"Say no more. Put your leg up here." Doing as I was told, I held onto the countertop to brace myself. "Fuck, Paris, this pussy good!" Jinx moaned, sliding back inside of me.

"Yess! Beat it up! Please don't stop!"

"Throw that ass back on this dick!" Standing on one leg, I bounced my ass back hard on him. "That's what the fuck I'm talking about, get that dick, Paris," he whispered in my ears, sending chills down my spine.

Ding Dong! Ding Dong!

"I'm about to cum again! Ahhhh shit, yes!"

"You finna make a nigga nut if you keep fucking me back like that," he groaned, getting a tight grip on my hair. I continued bouncing my ass in a circular motion while holding on to the counter.

"I'm about to cum fuck! I'm about to cum Jinx, don't stop!"

"Paris I'm cumming witcha, fuck!" he hollered, just as my orgasm hit me, causing me to lose my grip on the counter.

"Paris, what the fuck? You didn't hear Dream ringing the..." Lundyn stopped talking mid-sentence, locking eyes with me. "I know you fucking lying!" She laughed, as Jinx and I went falling to the floor after losing our balance.

"Paris Monroe! I leave for a few days, come back, you got a whole boo, and y'all fucking. I need a drink!" Dream shook her head, turning to walk out of the kitchen.

"Talk about embarrassing!"

Standing to my feet, I shook my head in shame while pulling my dress down. That's when I looked over to my left and saw Gunna laughing so hard he had tears running down his face. I couldn't do anything but laugh as I took the walk of shame to my bedroom.

*

"Paris!"

"What did I tell you about scaring me like that, damn Jinx?" I screamed when he pulled the shower curtain back stepping inside the shower with me.

"You just gone leave me in there by myself and not give me nothing to clean my dick off with?" He hissed, pushing me back up against the wall in the shower.

"I'm sorry, boo. I promise it wasn't intentional. I was trying to get up out of there. That was so embarrassing."

"Do you regret it?"

"Not at all, I wish everybody would leave so that we could go for round two."

"Is that right," he smirked, leaning down to kiss my lips.

"I'm so serious."

Stepping out of the shower, I went to grab a fresh washcloth for Jinx to wash up with.

"Let's hurry and freshen up so that we can get out of here. You're going to have to use my body wash because I don't keep nothing but girly soaps in my bathroom, love," I teased, passing him my Victoria Secret body wash.

"As long as my nuts clean, it's cool."

After I finished washing up, I rinsed off in a hurry then got out of the shower leaving Jinx alone with his thoughts. He still hadn't come out of the bathroom after I changed my clothes, so I headed back downstairs to get started on the food.

"Hey Paris, you look good friend!" Dream super bubbly self smiled, getting out of her seat to come hug me when I reached the bottom of the stairs.

"Hey bitch, I missed you."

"I know I missed you too, Paris. Do you need help cooking this food because I'm starving?"

"Nah, I got it boo. Before you get mad, I want you to know my boo invited his brother over to keep you company. Please don't embarrass me being a bitch, Dream."

"Damn, Paris! You know I don't do hookups. Niggas always bring the friend nobody wants to fuck with to keep you company." She sighed, rolling her eyes.

"I've seen a few of his people, and although they are a little rough around the edges, they are all fine as hell."

"Rough? Oh Lord, *issa thug*," she teased.

"Girl, straight savage is more like it. I'm not even going to stand here and lie to you."

"If I have to take one for the team, I will, but you better be ready to spill this tea. Not only do you have a new boo, but y'all fuckin'. Is this the same guy from the club, the night of my birthday? I need details, bitch." She laughed, taking a seat on the couch.

"That was Jinx. Yes, it's the same guy from the club. I'll introduce y'all when he comes back downstairs."

"Aye, Paris why you ain't tell me you were coming downstairs? I've been upstairs waiting on you!" Jinx snapped, walking up on me and wrapping his arms around my waist from behind.

"My bad you were still in the bathroom, so I came back down here to wait on you. Did you forget I had company?"

"It's cool, just say something next time."

"I got you. Jinx, this is my bestie Dream. Dream, this is my um... my friend Jinx."

"I'm her man, lil mama. Don't let her fool you. What up?" Jinx smiled, introducing himself.

"Damn Paris, you did good friend. I come back from out of town for a few days, and you got a whole ass man now." She laughed, being sarcastic.

"Jinx is my friend. We're just chillin' so relax, boo."

"I'm just saying. The Paris I'm used to is always too worried about her family to focus on the cobwebs that I'm sure need dusting off that coochie."

"Dream, oh my god, will you shut up!" I whined feeling embarrassed again.

"I'm just saying, Paris." Dream shrugged, walking off into the kitchen. When she was out of sight, Jinx pulled me to him.

"What she talking about, Paris?"

"She's making fun of me because I haven't had sex in a long time."

"Until today." He smiled before kissing me. "Paris, that pussy was umm, umm, good."

"Bye, Jinx." Blushing, I broke away from his hold. "Let me go in here and cook this food."

"My bro should be here soon, so I'm going to go wait on him. Give me a kiss."

"Ummm," I moaned, loving the way his lips felt. "Let me get started with dinner. Go, make yourself comfortable."

"I will. Can you bring me a drink when you get a chance?"

"I got you, boo."

Chapter Sixteen

JINX

I watched Paris as she walked away. The jeans she had on fit her slim-thick frame like a glove. I had to resist the urge to bend her over and fuck the shit out of her right here on the couch. Paris was cool as fuck. Talking on the phone every day and spending time with her was cool. However, that wasn't enough for me. I needed more. Women throw themselves at me on the regular, and I could fuck most of them if I wanted to, but for some reason, I was only feeling Paris right now.

I'm able to talk about shit other than shoes and bags with her. She listens to what a nigga has to say, and I appreciated that shit. Sometimes after a long day of chasing the bag, I want to go home to a home cooked meal, lay up, and get my dick sucked afterwards. I couldn't do that type of shit with the sack chasers I've fucked with in the past. That's why none of them has ever been to my crib. Paris is different though, and whether she knew it yet or not, she was stuck with a nigga after letting me fuck today.

"Jinx, I made you a drink." Paris smiled, passing me a cup.

"What's this, ma?"

"Patrón mixed with pineapple and orange juice."

"Come here, Paris."

"What's up, boo?" I pulled her down into my lap, careful not to spill my drink.

"Patrón keeps my dick hard, so if you don't want the taste licked off your pussy, then I suggest you don't give me anymore," I warned, planting kisses down her neck making her body tremble.

"Damn Jinx, what has gotten into you?" she moaned, breathlessly.

"You Paris, I'm just giving you the heads up."

Ding Dong!

"Someone is at the door, let me get that." She kissed my cheek then got off my lap.

"That's probably my brother. Let him in." She looked through the peephole to see who was standing there.

"I doubt this is your brother standing at the door." She had a confused expression on her face.

"That's him. He texted me not too long ago saying that he was almost here. Open the door for him. When she pulled the door open, she turned to look at me.

"What's up, lil mama? My name is Tommy Davis, but everybody calls me White Boy. I'm looking for my bro Jinx, is he here?"

"Yeah, he's here come inside. My name is Paris, by the way, nice to meet you."

"Likewise ma, you bad as fuck."

Aye bro, don't be pushing up on her. That's all me." I laughed getting up off the couch.

"How'd you get her to talk to yo ugly ass, bro?" White Boy asked, with a smirk on his face. I gave him a brotherly hug.

"Fuck you, White Boy. I'm glad you could stop by on short notice. This is my girl. She already told you her name, so there's no need to introduce y'all again."

"What's going on in here? Why y'all so damn loud?" Dream fussed, walking in the room.

"Dream, this is my bro Tommy, aka White Boy."

"Wait a minute, how is this your brother and he's white as snow? I know I've been drinking, but this is a white man."

"Dream!" Paris yelled, cutting her off.

I just laughed because I was used to the reaction from people whenever they met White Boy for the first time and I tell them he's my brother. He may have had white skin and a different blood type then me running through his veins, but you couldn't convince me that he wasn't my brother. We had been through the same struggles in life with the same fucked up kind of parents who left us as orphans.

"Nah, it's cool, I get this a lot. Blood doesn't make you family, lil mama, bonds and loyalty do. Jinx is definitely my brother. Don't get shit twisted."

All I could do was laugh. White Boy has been the same way since I met him when I was a young little nigga. Ain't shit changed but his age, financial status, and now he's covered in tattoos. White Boy was a savage just like me, not to mention he is a significant part of my drug operation. He is one of my best shooters after Gunna and a beast with this technology shit. He could hack into any computer system and get info on just about anyone in a matter of minutes. When that shooting happened at Club Reign, White Boy hacked into the club's security system, wiping out the entire system. Afterwards, he distorted every surveillance system within a ten-mile radius of the club so that the murder wouldn't fall back on us.

"Dream, why don't you keep my boy company while I help Paris finish cooking," I suggested.

"I guess I'll be a good sport Jinx, but only because I haven't seen my friend smile like this in a very long time."

"White Boy, I'll be in the kitchen holla if you need me."

"Is there somewhere I can smoke at?" he asked Paris.

"There's an area by the pool in the backyard. Dream will show you," Paris replied before turning to walk in the kitchen.

Chapter Seventeen

DREAM

L eading Tommy out to the backyard, I don't know why I felt nervous all of a sudden. I'm never the shy type, but here I was fidgeting like a fiend and stumbling over my words.

"It's nice out here. What was your name again?"

"It's Dream. Dream Davidson, Tommy, right?"

"Yeah, but I'm used to being called White Boy." He chuckled, sparking his blunt up. "You smoke?" he asked, lustfully roaming his beautiful green eyes all over my body from head to toe.

"Yeah, just a little bit. It doesn't offend you when people call you White Boy?" I asked, returning the same lustful stare.

"When I was a kid, it did. It was a name people used to say when teasing me. Somehow, my foster mother Ms. Deb taught me to embrace it in a sense. I grew up in the hood predominately around black folks. I never thought anything of it. I just looked at everyone like family cause we all got along for the most part. However, you know there's always that one negative ass person with something to say about me who was always hanging with people who didn't like me.

Anyway, to make a long story short, this kid name Marcus was always fucking with me, calling me *white boy*. I would always get mad, and we would end up fighting. After the third time beating his ass, Ms.

Deb, the lady who ran the group home, sat me down and had a talk with me. She just basically told me with me being white someone will always have something to say about me because they think I'm trying to be something that I'm not when honestly I'm just being myself. She started calling me White Beezy short for White Boy, and there was nothing negative behind it. My bros started calling me White Boy after, and the name just stuck. The rest is history," he explained, passing me the blunt.

"When I saw you my first thought was who is this fine ass tatted up white man. Just by your demeanor, I knew off top you grew up in the hood your entire life." I laughed, passing the blunt back after taking two pulls.

"Shit, I did grow up in the hood. I no longer give a fuck about how muthafuckas feel about me. I am who I am, and if a person don't like it, then fuck' em," He shrugged, staring up at the sun that was setting.

"I hope I didn't offend you."

"Nah, you good. I'm cooling, enjoying this beautiful Cali weather. What's up with you though? Since they basically putting us off on each other, I guess we should get to know each other," he teased, passing the blunt back to me. "You and my bro's girl are best friends?"

"Yeah, Paris and I have been friends since we were kids. Our fathers were business associates. It's been a long time since I've seen her smile. That's all she's been doing since I got here."

"Jinx is a real one. He doesn't rock like this with females, so he must like Paris."

"You think so?"

"Definitely. Enough about them, tell me about you. Where's your man at?"

"I don't have one. I have an ex that I'm still cool with, but other than that, I'm single."

"So basically, he still smashing?"

"Only when I'm in the mood."

"I respect your honesty."

"There's no sense in me lying about it."

"Facts," he agreed, nodding his head up and down. "You got any kids?"

"My son died four years ago when he was three months old."

"Damn, I'm sorry to hear that. I didn't know."

"How could you know, it's ok. I know he's watching over me."

"You better know it, Dream."

"Do you have any kids?"

"Nah, not yet. I want some eventually, but I haven't found me a chick that's wifey material yet."

"You don't have to be married to have kids, Tommy."

"Shit, I do. I don't want my kids to grow up in a home without both parents."

"Well now that you put it like that, I get where you're coming from."

"What you do for a living?"

"I'm a realtor, but eventually, I want to open my own business."

"You should. The housing market is starting to pick up again."

"I sell commercial units as well."

"That's what's up. Do you got a business card? I've been thinking about starting a business too. When it comes to computers and technology, there ain't much I can't do."

"That's dope. I'll give you my card whenever we go back inside. What type of business do you want to start?"

"I'm working on some security software that's top of the line. I want to sell my product to home and business owners."

"Go for it, Tommy. I think that's a great idea."

"You cool as fuck, Dream."

"You're not so bad yourself." I smiled staring into his handsome face, feeling flutters in my stomach.

"You straight?"

"Yeah, we should probably get ready to head back inside. It's getting dark out here."

"Lead the way," he smirked, ashing his blunt before tossing it into the trash.

Walking back into the kitchen, Paris was sitting on Jinx's lap playing with his beard while Lundyn and Gunna went back and forth talking shit to each other.

"What y'all got going on in here, Paris?"

"Girl, listening to these two fools argue about nothing."

"What happened?"

"Lundyn says they aren't in a relationship, but Gunna says that's a lie."

"Y'all are childish as hell. What is this high school?" I teased.

"Man, shut yo big head ass up. I was wondering why the sun set all of a sudden, and then here you come walking in the house forehead first!" Gunna's rude ass laughed.

"I swear you get on my nerves. I see why Lundyn doesn't want your ass. I like Rasheed better, Lundyn," I smirked, pissing Gunna off.

"Gunna, chill out bro. Don't even say shit," Tommy came to my defense.

"Nah fuck that! That shit wasn't funny bro."

"It was just a joke Gunna relax," White Boy said, trying to diffuse the situation.

"Gunna, baby, let's go outside and get in the pool. I'm about to go put my swimsuit on. Come help me find the perfect one," Lundyn grabbed him by the hand, leading him to her bedroom.

"Best friend, why did you go and say that dumb shit? You know Gunna's not working with a full deck," Paris asked when they were out of sight.

"I was just playing, my bad y'all."

"He will be alright," Tommy added.

"Everybody just move on. It's not that big of a deal. The food is almost ready," Paris said, changing the subject.

"I want to get in the pool with Lundyn."

"Do you have a swimsuit?" Paris inquired.

"Yeah, I have one of my bags in my trunk that I brought back from Jamaica."

"Well, go get it and change into it. When the food comes out of the oven, I'll go change into mine."

"Alright, I'll be right back."

Chapter Eighteen
PARIS

It was now a little after ten at night, and we were all drunk coupled off in my backyard. Jinx and I were in the Jacuzzi drinking Patrón vibin' to Nipsey Hussle's *Victory Lap* album playing in the background over my Bluetooth sound system. Lundyn and Gunna were in the pool cuddled up, while Dream and White Boy were off to the side playing cards, talking and doing their own thing.

"Paris I ain't never been able to just vibe with a chick like we doing right now," Jinx confessed, wrapping his arms around my body.

"I'm having a good time tonight chilling with you. I'm glad we met, and our family is getting along with each other."

"I am too. Gunna and Lundyn need couple's therapy though." He laughed.

"Let my sister tell it they're not in a relationship."

"Shitttt, look at them over there." He laughed, pointing in their direction. "That looks like some shit only couples should be doing."

Gunna had Lundyn on the shallow end of the pool reaching for shit that wasn't there. I could tell he was giving her nasty ass dick from behind while they were in the pool.

"They need to take that shit in the house."

"They are grown, Paris. We got our own thing going on over here to be worrying about, baby sis getting them guts beat up." Turning around, I picked my drink up off the edge of the Jacuzzi, taking a sip while straddling Jinx's lap.

"You're right we got our own thing going on over here."

"You probably should stop drinking, or you're not going to be able to go to work in the morning."

"I'm in the office tomorrow doing paperwork, so I don't have to be in until noon."

"Well, in that case, you got time to give me some more pussy."

"Let's go to my bedroom."

"No, we chillin', can't nobody see what we doing in this Jacuzzi. Just focus on me." Jinx released his dick from his boxers in one quick motion, while pulling my bikini bottom to the side.

"Wh-what are you—"

"Shhh, let me take care of you," he replied, lifting me and sliding me down on his dick.

"Sssssshit!" I moaned aloud, throwing my head back.

"Be quiet, Paris." Jinx shut me up, covering my lips with his. With my arms around his neck, I slammed up and down his pole splashing water everywhere.

"It feels so good."

"Ride that dick! Yo fine ass is working that pussy!" In minutes, I was calling out his name having my first orgasm.

"I'm about to cum! Ahh yessss, Jinx!" I released a low moan, trying to be discreet.

"Wet my dick up!" Jinx commanded, wrapping his hands around my neck, squeezing lightly. "Let it go, Paris! Wet my dick up!"

On command, I came all over him. He held me in place pounding me from underneath until he came right after me. I could barely focus as I tried to catch my breath.

"Damn, bestie you and Lundyn are nasty, nasty! Y'all should have made a movie!" Dream yelled from the other side of my backyard, cracking up laughing.

"Bitch, you sound big mad!" Lundyn yelled back at Dream. I

couldn't say a word if I wanted to. Jinx had put me in a dick coma as I laid my head on his chest with my eyes closed.

"Paris! Baby, I know you're not going to sleep out here." Jinx laughed, planting soft kisses on my forehead, as I drifted off to sleep.

Chapter Nineteen

JINX

Two Weeks Later

I had just finished making my rounds checking on my marijuana dispensaries so that I could go to lunch with Paris when I got a call from Devon telling me he needed me to get to his house quick. He said he needed help with his mother. I really wasn't in the mood to be dealing with Keisha's bullshit this morning, but since I had a soft spot for Devon, and it was just around the corner, I went anyway. Pulling up to Devon's apartment building, I hopped out the car making sure my pistol was secure on my waistline. After climbing two flights of stairs, I knocked at the door then waited on someone to answer.

Knock! Knock!

Seconds later, a pissed off Devon pulled the door open. I stepped inside then locked the door behind me.

"What's going on, D?"

"She's in here, follow me, Jinx." Mobbin' into his mother's bedroom, Keisha was laid out on her back looking a hot ass mess.

"What's wrong with her, D?"

"I don't know. I've been trying to wake her up for twenty minutes, but she won't wake up."

Walking over to Keisha's bedside, I checked her pulse. She had a steady pulse, so I knew the bitch wasn't dead.

"Go bring me a big pot filled to the brim with warm water. Not too cold, but not hot to the point you burn someone."

"Ok, give me a minute."

While I waited, I checked the time. Paris should be calling me at any minute now, so I needed to hurry and wrap this shit up.

"Here's the water Jinx. What are you about to do?"

"Step back, Devon."

As soon as he stepped back out of the way, I tossed the entire pot of water on Keisha's powda head ass. She jumped up immediately screaming and grabbing for shit that wasn't there thinking that she was drowning.

"Ahhhh, what the fuck! Why did you throw water on me, Jinx?"

"Mom, don't be mad at him. I've been trying to wake you up for almost twenty minutes."

"I was sleep, Devon, damn!"

"Devon, step out of the room! Go check on your brother and sister. I need to holla at yo mama real quick!"

"Bro, you are not about to hurt my mama!"

"Nigga, if I was gone hurt yo mama what the fuck was you gone do about it? I just want to talk to her unfit ass!"

"Don't hurt my mother, Jinx," Devon warned, backing out the room.

"Keisha, get yo funky goat smelling ass up and get in the shower before I send some of the home girls over here to beat yo ass! You got this room smelling like week old pussy and onion juice. Them fuckin' kids are in there raising themselves while yo is ass sleeping till almost three o'clock in the afternoon. Bitch, get the fuck up!"

"Fuck you, Jinx! My kids are well taken care of."

"Only because of Devon, not because of yo smut ass!"

"What you need to do is get the fuck out my house before I call the police on your black ass!"

"Keisha, I'm only gone say this shit once. Watch how you talk to me!"

"You got some nerve!" she yelled at me.

"I don't give a fuck about nothing but them kids in there! Get yo ass up, get in the shower, and then put some fucking clothes on. You got twenty minutes to bring your ass out of the room. Oh yeah, and if you ever talk to me like you just did again, you won't like what I'ma do to you!" I warned her.

"Fine Jinx, I'm sorry. Now get out! I will be out in a minute. Now please just get out!"

I gladly walked out of the room then went to check on the kids. They were sitting at the table eating lunch that Devon made. It felt good to see them laughing and carrying on without a care in the world. Watching these kids made me have so much more respect for Devon because through his mother's neglect and addiction, he still found a way to keep a smile on his brother and sister faces.

Knock! Knock!

"Devon, get the door." He came running back to me seconds later.

"Jinx, the social worker is at the door. What am I gone do?"

"Go stall her while I go get your mama."

"Ok, hurry up," I ran to the back busting in the bedroom without knocking. Keisha was standing there asshole naked. She didn't even bother covering up when she saw me standing there.

"Jinx, what the fuck are you doing? If you wanted some pussy, all you had to do was ask," she purred, licking her dry ass lips.

"Girl, I don't want that ran through ass pussy. Hurry up and put some clothes. Devon said the social worker is at the door."

"Oh my god, I'm so sick of them people popping up at my house fucking with me. There ain't even no food in there for them kids to eat."

"Just put some clothes on and come in the living room. Devon is out there stalling."

"I'm coming, Jinx." When I walked back into the living room, I was immediately confused.

"Paris, what are you doing here? I told you to call me when you made it on this side of town so that we could grab lunch."

"I'm sorry, Jinx, but I'm here to do a home visit. This is strictly business. I was going to call you after I left here."

"Hi, Ms. Monroe. I didn't know we had a scheduled visit today." Keisha smiled, walking out the room with workout clothes on. "I just came in from the gym. I'm so glad you came after I made it back home," she lied.

"Ms. Moore, this isn't a scheduled home visit. I'm here because it's been reported that your daughter Desi has been missing at least one day of school every week before school was let out for the summer. In order for these children to remain in your custody, she has to go to school every day during the school year unless a licensed professional excuses it. You have a court date in two months, and if things don't change soon, then I'll have to recommend that the children be removed from your care."

"Ms. Monroe, that won't be necessary." I smiled, walking over to Paris. "I guarantee you that Ms. Moore here will have all of her children in school every day when school starts back in a few weeks after the summer break. Isn't that right, Keisha?" I lied, giving her a look so cold she took two steps back.

"Ye-yes, that's right, Ms. Monroe, all of my kids will be in school every day."

"Now that we have that understood, I need to check the kitchen before I leave to make sure there is food to eat."

"I was just about to go shopping Ms. Monroe."

"I still have to check, Ms. Moore. It's standard protocol."

Walking into the kitchen, Paris opened the cabinets that were filled with can goods, snacks, and boxes of cereal. The refrigerator was filled from top to bottom with food. Devon looked at me smiling. Right then, I knew that he had bought groceries with the money I give him every Friday.

"Well, everything looks fine here, so I'm gonna go on and get out of here."

"Ok, thanks for stopping by Ms. Monroe." Keisha gave a fake smile walking Paris to the door. After making sure Paris was gone, she turned to me.

"Oh my god, that was close. I have to get myself together," she cried.

Devon ran to his mother, wrapping his arms around her. For him to be only fourteen, he stood almost six feet tall towering over her small frame.

"Keisha, I know I be hard on you, but it's only because of these kids. I remember who you were before the partying and before the drugs. Your husband was one of the old heads I respected a lot growing up. If he could see you now, I know for a fact it would fuck him up seeing the person you've become. You need to make a change before you get these kids put in the system!" I snapped, before walking out the house, slamming the door behind me. As soon as I got back to my car, I sparked the blunt sitting in the cup holder.

Ring! Ring!

I answered seeing that it was Paris calling.

"Yeah, what's up?"

"Ummm... is everything alright?"

"Yeah, I just need a minute to calm down. Where are you?"

"Sitting around the corner in my car in front of your store."

"Don't move, I'm about to pull up on you."

"See you soon, Jinx." I finished the blunt before I drove off. When I hit the block, all the homies was outside in front of my store.

"Ayoooo! Move the fuck out the way so that I can park my shit!" I yelled, hanging out of the window. Once they saw that it was me, everybody moved their cars out of the middle of the street so that I could park.

"What up, nigga?" I bobbed my head at Gunna who was standing outside hugged up with Lundyn. Walking around to the passenger side of Lundyn's car where Paris was sitting, I opened the door. "What's up, ma?"

"Hey Jinx, where is your car?"

"It's a few cars back."

"Are you ready to get some food? I'm starving."

"I can't believe you're Devon's caseworker. It's a small world."

"It definitely is. Let's head to my car so that we can go to lunch before I have to get back to work."

"I'm right behind you, just let me go say what's up to Gunna."

"Hurry up, Jinx."

"Man, take yo fine ass to the car. I said, I'm coming!" After checking on Gunna making sure he was good, I headed to the car with Paris who was sitting in the passenger seat with an attitude.

"It took you long enough. I told you I had to get back to work soon!"

"Man, calm yo ass down! You must need some act right, is that what the problem is?" I snapped, getting behind the wheel of her G-Wagon.

"Thanks for driving, my damn feet hurt."

"No problem, but what's with the attitude?"

"I'm over it. Let's just go get some food. I'm starving," she expressed, leaning over to kiss my cheek. Grabbing her by the chin, I tongued her pretty ass down before starting the car.

"Damn," she moaned breathlessly, falling back in the seat dramatically.

"You so extra." I laughed, placing my hand on her thick thigh as I pulled off. "Where do you want to eat?"

"I got a taste for some fish. Let's go to this spot on Crenshaw and 109th. They have really good seafood."

"I thought you were trying to go to a restaurant."

"I wanted to, but I have to get back to work soon. As long as I eat, I'll be happy."

"Greedy ass!" I teased.

"Team greedy all day." She laughed, being silly.

It took me fifteen minutes to make it to Inglewood where the fish spot was. This wasn't my neck of the woods, so I planned to be in and out. After finding a place to park, we got out the car heading inside.

"I already know what I want so whenever you're ready we can order."

"I want the seafood platter with extra hush puppies. What are you getting?"

"I want the shrimp platter and an order of fried oysters with a Sprite."

"I got you."

After placing our orders, Paris wanted to go to the sneaker spot that was next door to look around. She found a few pairs of Jordan's she liked, so I got them all for her and a couple of pairs for myself.

As we were leaving to get our food from next door, I saw a chick named Shaneka I used to fuck with standing outside the fish spot. I cut her off about five months ago because her ratchet ways were too much for a nigga. Now every time she sees me, she acts a damn fool. Shaneka was pretty but ghetto as fuck and had nothing going for herself, so I had to cut her off.

"Well, well, well! What's up, Jinx?" Shaneka smirked while licking her lips lustfully at me. "Is this bitch the reason you stopped checking for me? I mean she cute and all, but she could NEVER be me!"

"Man, gone with that bullshit! I'm not on that shit right now."

"Baby, our food is ready. Let's go before it gets cold." Paris grabbed my hand, pulling me away, trying to diffuse the situation. "Just ignore her. she's a bird doing what they do best— chirping!" She smiled, looking up at me.

Leaning down, I kissed her lips twice before walking back inside the food spot.

Before we could reach the counter, the sound of glass breaking caught my attention. *Bam! Bam! Bam!*

"Yeah nigga, I want you to remember this moment next time you try to play me! Fuck you, Jinx!" Shaneka yelled, swinging a metal bat busting the windows out of Paris's G-Wagon.

"Ahh hell nah! You know I'm about to fuck this hoe up right, Jinx? I work too hard for mine!" Paris snapped, running out the door to confront Shaneka.

She was throwing her hands like a skilled boxer, connecting every hit. After letting her get a few licks in, I was able to grab ahold of her right after she swung twice hitting Shaneka in both eyes swelling them instantly.

"Don't let the business suit and pretty face fool you! I will drag your ass bitch!"

"Paris calm down, lil mama. You fucked her up good, so chill out," I hissed in Paris' ear, while she fought with all her strength trying to break free.

"Let me go, Jinx! I don't do this type of shit anymore. You got me out here acting a fool because you can't control your bitches!"

"Paris, calm that shit down! Shaneka ain't my bitch!"

"Bitch, don't you dance at Oasis?" Shaneka yelled. "You ain't nothing but a piece of pussy to this nigga, trust me! I may be ghetto, but at least I'm not a stripper hoe! I heard how you bitches get down in the VIP rooms," Shaneka laughed, holding her right eye with her hand.

"Let me go Jinx so that I can fuck this hoe up again!"

"Paris, calm the fuck down! Look at me!"

"Please let me go so that I can beat her ass, Jinx!" she begged, looking up at me with pleading eyes.

"Fuck her, Paris! Calm the fuck down so that we can get our food and go. If you show your ass, I promise I'm gone fuck you clean up!" I warned through clenched teeth.

"Fine, but let me in the car, or I swear to God I'm going to jail for killing this hoe!"

Walking Paris backwards to the car, I opened the door through the broken window. After helping her inside, I made Shaneka leave after snatching her ass up putting her in the car, forcing her to drive off. By the time I got to the food, it was cold, so the entire way to drop Paris' car off at my homies car shop, she bitched and complained about how nasty the food was. It was bad enough Shaneka had fucked her car up now she wouldn't shut the fuck up about the cold food. My nerves were so bad that I was on edge.

"Where are we at? I swear to God you got me so mad right now."

"Look, Paris! What happened back there wasn't my fault. Shaneka was just trying to be seen. I hadn't fucked with that bitch in months, long before I met you."

"That's not the point, Jinx. I got too much to lose to be dealing with this type of drama! I should never have to drag a bitch in the middle of a parking lot while I'm on my lunch break, especially over a nigga!"

"Man, shut that shit up! You be killing me with that Ms. Goody two shoes bullshit! You walking around carrying a loaded pistol in your designer bag while you're at work, and you mad talking to me about fighting a bitch that doesn't even mean shit to me? Man, get the fuck out of here!" I snapped, getting out the car slamming the door behind me.

I walked off pacing the parking lot, trying to calm down before I said and did something I might regret later on.

"You know Jinx maybe this isn't going to work out between us. It's obvious you have some loose ends you need to tie up, so I'll just go."

Then leave shit! You won't be the first muthafucka to walk out of my life so if it's that serious, just go! Get the fuck on!" I yelled in frustration.

"I called me an Uber, and it's two minutes away. I'll call you in a few days when I figure out what I want to do about my car," she explained, taking her tote with her case files out of the trunk.

I didn't even bother to respond. I sparked me a blunt watching her from a distance until she got in the back seat of her Uber and drove away.

Chapter Twenty

PARIS

One Month Later

I t was bright and early on a Friday morning when my alarm went off waking me up. I was still tired with a pounding headache, feeling like I needed to lie back down for a few more hours of sleep. Although I was tired, I got up dragging myself out of bed into the bathroom to get ready for work.

After stopping by Starbucks to get a cup of coffee, I headed to the first location on my list of clients houses I had to see today. It was the end of summer, and all the kids were still out of school running up and down the streets having water fights. That brought back so many memories from my childhood. Every summer, my dad would throw pool parties in our backyard and invite all his friends and their kids over. We would have the time of our lives.

Ring! Ring!

My phone started ringing when I pulled in front of my client's apartment in Long Beach, California. Without checking to see who was calling, I answered the phone.

"Hello."

"What's going on, princess?" I pulled the phone away from my ear, surprised to hear my father's voice. The last time we talked was months ago, and it wasn't on good terms.

"Oh, it's just you, dad. What's up?" I rolled my eyes, smacking my teeth in irritation.

"I got a new cell phone. I just wanted to give you the number."

"Well, thanks for the heads-up, dad."

"Have you thought about what we discussed the last time you came to visit me?"

"We haven't spoken to each other in over a month! It's crazy how instead of you asking if I'm good out here, shit or even asking how my sister is doing, you're only worried about yourself as usual!" I spat, rolling my eyes in irritation.

"Just answer the fucking question, Paris Monroe!"

"No, dad! I haven't even given it a second thought. There is no way I'm going to put my freedom on the line to do what you asked. I've seen what the end result is, and I want no parts of it!"

"That's your word?" He laughed, being sarcastic.

"I've said all I have to say."

"You ungrateful bitch!"

"Excuse me!"

"You heard what the fuck I said. I spent years getting my hands dirty while you reaped the benefits of my grind and hustle. You mean to tell me that doesn't mean shit to you? You can't look out for your old man when I need you?"

"Don't you dare try and make me feel guilty because of your life choices! I was a child! It was your responsibility to take care of me! I never asked to be here!"

"Could your sudden change of attitude have anything to do with this new nigga, I hear you're running around town with? You do know I keep my ears to the street, don't you?"

"Newsflash you selfish muthafucka, these last six years that you and mom have been locked up it's been me Paris Monroe keeping your commissary stacked, paying for packages, and doing everything you've asked of me and then some! Not only did I do this shit for you, but mom too! Do you think that shit is cheap?"

"You owe me. That's the least you could do!" he hissed, into the phone.

"Are you fucking serious right now, dad? I don't owe anybody shit. I degraded myself for years shaking my ass for cash to make sure this entire family could live a lifestyle we were somewhat accustomed to. I had to help finish raising my little sister when I was just a teenager my damn self! All because your ass got my mother caught up in your bull-shit and both of my parents ended up behind bars. I never complained. I never uttered one word. I got out there and made shit happen because I had nobody else looking out for me! This is the thanks I get? How about this, fuck you, dad! And since you don't appreciate all I've done for you over the years, you make sure to stretch that last three thousand dollars I sent you last week until you come home. You got me fucked up straight up."

"Play with me if you want to, and I'll have your ass touched. You remember what happened to Quincy, right? You don't want that to happen again, do you?" He laughed, menacingly into the phone. "You got seven days to get back with me, and when I call, you better be ready to go pick up that work from an old friend of mine. I'm done playing games with you, Paris!"

I was still stuck on what he said about Quincy because he had nothing to do with this conversation.

"What exactly are you trying to say about Quincy?" I asked, breaking my silence. "Are you threatening me?"

"Seven days Paris, I'm done playing games with you."

"Answer me you piece of shit!"

"I'll be in touch!"

Click!

After my dad hung up in my face, I sat in my rental car shaking I was so upset. I was really trying not to allow him to get to me, but I was legit in my feelings all over again. I had been putting the last argu-ment between us into the back of my mind, trying to forget about it and praying the situation fixed itself, but that clearly wasn't going to happen. I now wanted to know exactly what he meant by the state-ment he made about Quincy. If I found out my own father had some-thing to do with his murder, he's good as dead to me.

While I sat in my car taking slow deep breaths to clear my head, I kept wondering what Jinx was up to or if I was on his mind. I hadn't talked to him in over a month since we got into that crazy argument over one of his ex-hoes. The first two weeks he had been calling and texting me about my car, that was being repaired by one of his homies every day, but I hadn't responded to any of his messages. The following two weeks I didn't hear from him at all. Because of my stubbornness, I had to been paying for a rental car for an entire month. Deciding to be the bigger person, I sent a short text to let him know I was thinking of him.

Me: I miss you.

After a few minutes went by, he replied.

Jinx: Prove it. Meet me for dinner tonight.

Me: Can I cook for you? It's Friday, and I want to unwind after work.

Jinx: That's cool. Come to my house and cook. I won't be home till about nine, but I'll have Mama G let you in.

Me: Are you sure? I can wait until you get home.

Jinx: Nah it's cool. Mama G will keep you company until I get there.

Me: Ok. What do you want me to cook?

Jinx: Surprise me.

Me: Ok, I got you.

Jinx: Paris...

Me: Yeah, what's up?

Jinx: I miss you too. I apologize for how I talked to you. I should have handled the situation differently.

Me: Prove it.

Jinx: Say less.

I didn't realize how much I missed Jinx until reading his text for the second time. I sat in the car for another ten minutes before I realized I wasted enough time daydreaming, so I got out of the car and headed to my client's house. After spending almost an hour inside with my clients, I left satisfied with the outcome of my visit. Nothing made me happier than helping a child be placed in a home with a loving family who actually cared about them. This particular family actually adopted two little boys whose parents died in a car accident last year. To see how well adjusted the boys were to their new environment made my day.

Hours later, after another long day of work, I pulled up to my house, parked, then headed inside to pack a bag for the night. Walking into my bedroom, I stripped down out of my clothes then fell back on my bed.

"Hey sis, I thought I heard you come in. How was work?" Lundyn asked, walking in my room sitting down on my bed.

"What up boo, work was work. I'm tired, I know that much. I have to get me some new vitamins or something because my energy has been so low lately."

"Maybe because you've been eating everything in sight ever since you stop talking to Jinx."

"I texted him today."

"You did? How did that go?"

"I'm going to his house tonight to cook dinner for him."

"Whatttttt?" Lundyn laughed, dragging her words. "I'm glad y'all finally had a conversation. Gunna told me just last night how bad Jinx's been snapping on everyone around him ever since you stop talking to him. Apparently, the nigga's been on a rampage since you cut him off from that good ole Monroe pussy."

"Bye, Lundyn! I'm not about to play with you," I laughed, playfully hitting her arm. "You don't have a lick of sense, sis."

"I'm just saying." She shrugged, standing up from the bed.

"I talked to your father today."

"My father? Oh Lord, what he do now?"

"Still on that same shit. He threatened me again. He said I had seven days to change my mind, or he would have me touched."

"Paris, please tell me you're lying!"

"No, I wish I was lying. He even knew I had been dealing with Jinx."

"How did he know that? You haven't seen Jinx in like what ... over a month now, right?"

"Yep just a little over a month, but that's beside the point. He got niggas out here checking for me, and I don't like that. He may be acting like a bitch right now, but we have to keep in mind he knows a lot of people that probably owe him favors."

"Are you scared he will really have someone hurt you?"

"Honestly I'm not sure anymore. The man who called me today wasn't my father. That was, The Don, the nigga the streets feared. The Don is capable of anything, so moving forward we both need to be on alert."

"I'm always strapped just like you taught me. Our guns are registered, so let a nigga run up if they want to."

"That part! It's just sad I even have to worry about my father trying to harm me."

"Maybe you should talk to Jinx about it and see what he thinks you should do."

"I have to see how tonight goes. If everything works out, then I will tell him."

"What you cooking tonight? I might have to pull up and get me a plate."

"No, the fuck your not, boo. I'm trying to have some alone time with Jinx tonight."

"Basically, you're trying to get some dick?"

"Get out, hoe!" I laughed, getting up off the bed, walking in my closet to get my luggage.

"Well have fun tonight, sis. That makeup sex be the best sex, I'm trying to tell you."

"I promised myself that I was just going to go with the flow. I'm not going over there with high expectations. It's been a month now. A lot can change in a month."

"Stop overthinking the situation, and just enjoy your night. Make sure you make that nigga a meal he will never forget. Put some sexy shit on, make some drinks, and put on some good music. You can never go wrong with that."

"That sounds like a plan, Lundyn. Now get out so that I can take a quick shower before I leave. I still need to go to the market to get everything I'm going to need for dinner tonight."

"Well, don't let me hold you up. Make sure you freshen that coochie up. There's gone be a lot of eating and beating tonight, bihh!" She laughed, walking out the room. All I could do was shake my head at my sister's crazy ass. She had no chill whatsoever.

I grabbed everything needed then headed to the bathroom to take a shower. After getting the water temperature to my liking, I stepped inside the hot shower letting the water relax me. Emerging myself completely under the showerhead, my long hair immediately curled up to its natural state. I washed, conditioned, and then rinsed my hair, before cleaning my body washing the days stress away. Opening the door to the shower, I rubbed my wet feet on my plush rug then wrapped a towel around my wet hair and body before rushing inside my room to my ringing cell phone.

"Hello!"

"Aye, where you at?"

"I just got out the shower, about to get dressed. I need to stop by the market before I head to your house."

"Alright cool. I just wanted to tell you that Mama G knows your coming, so when you get there, shoot me a text. I will have her come out to let you in."

"Sounds good. I can't wait to see you," I confessed.

"I miss everything about you. Your annoying ass grew on a nigga. I promise to make up for the time we lost when I see you later."

"I look forward to it, boo." I smiled into the phone.

"I bet you are cheesing from ear to ear with dimples on full display. I miss your pretty ass."

"Let me get off this phone. I'll see you soon."

"I'm out handling business, but I'll be there as soon as I can."

"I'll be waiting. Goodbye, Jinx.

Click.

&

Pulling up to Jinx's house, I sat outside of the tall, iron gate surrounding his home waiting on Mama G to come out to let me in. After waiting about five minutes, she finally appeared in the driveway. She pressed the button on the remote for the gate, and it slowly opened. Driving the short path along the long circular driveway, I parked behind one of Jinx's cars then got out.

"Hey, Mama G, how are you?"

"Oh, I'm just fine, baby. I'm so happy to see you. Come on, let's go inside so that we can talk."

"I have to get my bags out of the trunk, and then I'll be right in."

"Let me help you with that."

"I got it, Mama G."

"Girl, don't be silly. I may be old, but I ain't cripple. Give me some of those bags so that we can go inside."

"If you insist." I shrugged, passing her two of the lighter bags.

I picked up the rest of them along with my overnight bag and then followed behind Mama G into the house and headed the kitchen. After placing everything on the table, I pulled out a chair and had a seat.

"Oh my god, those bags were heavy."

"You should have let me carry some more bags, child." Mama G laughed, removing the food from the bags placing everything on the counter in the middle of the kitchen. "Why don't you go take your bag upstairs to Jinx's room and then come back down so that we can chit-chat while you cook."

"Alright cool. I'll be right back."

When I entered Jinx's room, the smell of his cologne hit my nose, making me feel some type of way. I missed him so much. A white t-shirt was on the bed that Jinx must have left behind. Picking it up, I sniffed it appreciating the small shit like how good he always smelled. Placing my bag on the bed, I unzipped it getting a rubber band out of the side pocket putting my long curly hair in a ponytail then went back downstairs.

"Mama G!"

"I'm still in here, baby."

"Sorry if I took too long."

"Don't be silly. I have everything out that I thought you might need when you cook."

"Ok, thanks."

"What are you making?"

"Lobster tails, steak, cheesy mash potatoes, and roasted Brussel sprouts."

"That sounds good. I'm definitely getting me a plate." She laughed as she took a seat at the table.

"Can I ask you a question?"

"Sure, what is it?"

"How long have you known, Jinx?"

"All of his life. Why do you ask?"

"I don't know. I guess I just want to understand him better."

"Jinx is many things. He's rough around the edges, but he is also a good person with a heart of gold."

"That's what I like the most about him. There's more to him than just being a street nigga."

"The streets are all he knows Paris. If you like my boy the way I think you do, then you have to figure out a way to help him balance out the two."

"What do you mean?" I asked for clarity.

"Be the one who helps to bring light into his world of darkness if that makes sense."

"How can I do that? We talk about everything, but when it comes to certain things, he puts up a brick wall and won't let me all the way in. I know we haven't been dealing with each other for that long, but I really like him."

"Just keep doing whatever it is that you were doing with him. He needs love to cancel out all the darkness surrounding him. Be his peace.

"I think it has a lot to do with his hatred for his mother. He shuts completely down whenever I ask too many questions about her," I explained, getting a pot to boil my potatoes in.

"Let me tell you something. I want you to keep this between you and me."

"I promise I won't say a word to anyone."

"I'm only telling you this because I know in my heart you will be the woman Jinx marries one day."

"What! What makes you say that?"

"Chile, Jinx has been moping around here for weeks looking pathetic snapping on anyone who looked his way too long. He and Martez almost came to blows last week, and that's when I knew the love bug had bitten him." She smiled, getting up from her seat to get a bottle of wine and two glasses.

"Martez?"

"That's Gunna's name. Don't tell that nut I told you. You know he ain't wrapped too tight," she teased, passing me a glass of wine.

"Anyway, like I was saying. It wasn't until earlier today when you called him that I saw that glow in his eyes that has been missing since you two have been at odds."

"Are you serious?"

"I'm serious. Let me tell you what I wanted to talk to you about before it slips my mind."

"Ok I'm all ears," I called out over my shoulder, placing the pan with the steak in the oven.

"Come have a seat." Doing as I was told I had a seat across from Mama G then took a sip of my wine.

"Jinx has a hard time talking about his mother because she's never been a part of his world."

"He's told me that much."

"I'm sure he has, but what he didn't tell you was how it all started. She tossed him in the trash after giving birth to him."

"What!"

"Yes, child it's true. His mother was a mess, always has been. She gave my good friend, who was his grandmother, hell her entire life."

"What happened to her? How did she get that way?"

"I say it was her daddy's blood running through her veins. Tamika always attracted the wrong kind of people in her life. Once the streets got ahold of her, it was all downhill from there. She met Jinx's father, who was a low-level drug dealer. He started using his own product and talked Tamika into trying it. In less than a month, she was hooked."

"That's so sad."

"You had to be there. It was much worse to watch Tamika, who was a very beautiful girl, destroy her life. She was out there bad, Paris," Mama G explained, wiping a tear from her eye. "She got pregnant a few months down the line with Jinx. She wanted to get an abortion, but his father wouldn't allow her to do it. He locked her in the house for a month after that making her clean herself up and get that monkey off her back cold turkey. He was excited about the pregnancy. Tamika was pissed though. Her using heroin, which was her drug of choice, was more important to her than staying clean and sober for her unborn child."

"So, what happened next?"

"She was maybe just seven or eight months pregnant when she snuck off one night to score drugs."

"Who would sell drugs to a pregnant woman? Oh my god, that's crazy."

"That happens every day but let me finish. So his mother got the drugs, linked back up with some of her old friends, then went to get high. Shortly after her water broke and she went into labor in the alley behind the 110 freeway on Grand Avenue on the east side. Instead of calling 911 after she gave birth, she tossed him in the dumpster nearby and left."

"I couldn't imagine doing that to my child. How did he survive such a horrible situation?"

"Some kids walking that path home from school heard his cry and went to get their parents who found Jinx and rescued him. Once he was at the hospital, later that night Tamika ended up at the same place, after she passed out in front of the liquor store from losing too much blood. The nurses at the hospital figured it out after doing a blood test, and they were a perfect match."

By now, I had tears freely falling down my face imaging what that must feel like to have your mother discard you like a piece of trash.

"The worst part of this all was she named that boy Jinx."

"Why would she do that? That's so messed up he has to walk around with a crazy name like Jinx."

"I know baby it was terrible, but there was nothing anyone could do since she was technically the mother."

"She should have been arrested for abandoning her newborn baby!" I cried into my hands, feeling hurt for Jinx.

"The laws were different back then, Paris. The blessing in it all was the state allowed his grandmother Naomi to take him home with her once he was well enough to leave the hospital. She raised him the best she could, but Jinx was always into shit. He felt like he had to make life easier for his granny. I think he felt like a burden to her in a sense. When she couldn't afford to buy certain things or pay a bill, he would leave and come back hours later with the money for her. I knew he was robbing people for the money, but what could we do to stop him? Once he got arrested, he tried to turn things around, but shortly after Tamika got murdered for stealing drugs from one of them local drug dealers. Then his father, who he's never met went to prison for life for killing Tamika's murderer. After that, just a few short months later, Naomi had a massive stroke and died."

"That's a lot for any child to deal with all at once."

"It all happened within a year," Mama G explained, getting up to get a napkin then wiped at the tears running down my face. "Stop all this crying, baby girl. I only told you all of this to help you understand why Jinx is the way he is. If it's too much for you to handle, then walk away now. Don't wait until months down the line when he's madly in love with you then walk away. I don't think he will ever be the same if that were to happen."

"I wouldn't do that to him. We stopped talking over a silly disagreement."

"He asked me my opinion on the situation. I say you did the right thing until you blamed him for how you reacted."

"So, it was my fault?" I asked in disbelief while getting up to check on my potatoes.

"No, it wasn't your fault. The chick approached him was at fault, but it was your fault for reacting the way you did. You chose to take the bait. You gave her exactly what she wanted. She was jealous because she wanted to be the woman on Jinx's arm, but instead, it was you."

"She was a ratchet ass mess."

"That's the reason why you're in his house and not her. You're the first person he's ever brought home for me to meet in all these years I've been working for him."

"Are you serious?"

"As a heart attack. Look in that cabinet next to the stove and pass me that cheese grater so I can grate the cheese for you."

Doing as I was told, I handed everything to her before she started talking again.

"There must be something different about you if he likes you enough to trust you in his home when he's not here. He doesn't allow very many people to know where he lays his head. I know I've been running my mouth nonstop, but I just want you to know that all Jinx needs is love."

"I'll remember that going forward. Thanks for sharing this with me."

"You're welcome. All I ask is that you remember to keep this little talk between the two of us." She smiled as she grated the cheese.

"I promise. This stays between us."

"Thank you, baby. I'm all done here. Let me head back to the guesthouse. I know my boy will be here soon. I want to be as far away from you two as possible. I can only imagine what these walls will be able to see once you two pounce on each other," she teased.

"Mama G!" I laughed, so hard that I choked on my wine.

"What, child? I was once young." She smiled, walking out of the kitchen and leaving me to my thoughts.

Chapter Twenty-One

JINX

The smell of food hit me when I walked in the house, making my stomach grumble. I checked the time seeing it was a little after ten o'clock. I told Paris I would be here by nine, but I made a quick stop before getting here, and shit took longer than expected. This morning I got a new shipment of weed for my dispensaries, so I had to make my rounds checking to make sure shit was running smoothly. After another long day of grinding, I was ready to blow a few blunts back to back, eat some food, and hopefully make shit right with Paris. I was surprised when she texted me earlier because she had been avoiding me at all cost, so I was happy as fuck that she was even at my crib when I got home.

"Paris! Where you at?" I called out walking into the candlelit kitchen to find it empty. Walking up the stairs to my bedroom, she wasn't there either. "Paris! Baby where you at?"

After checking the family room seeing she wasn't there, I immediately went out on the deck searching for her. I found her sitting outside drinking a glass of wine staring off into space. This was one of my favorite spots in my house. I sat out here for hours some nights getting a peace of mind. Walking over to her, I picked her up, sitting down, placing her on my lap.

"Jinx you scared the shit out of me. I hate when you do that."

"My bad, you were zoned out."

"My mind drifted off, I guess."

"I like sitting out here sometimes too."

"Listening to the waves hit the shore is so peaceful, I could stay out here all night. What time is it? I wonder how long I've been out here."

"It's ten thirty. Sorry I got home so late, I—"

"Shhh! It's ok. I'm just glad you're here. I've missed you," she confessed, turning around straddling my lap. "I don't want to fight with you anymore. Let's start over." Grabbing both sides of my face, by my long beard, she kissed my lips softly.

Unable to resist her any longer, I grabbed her by the back of her neck, pulling her closer to me deepening the kiss. Her hands made their way down to my belt, unfastening my buckle in one quick motion. She released my dick from my boxers and then stood up, kicking her leggings off with urgency.

"You must really miss a nigga," I mumbled, stroking my dick staring at her fine ass with lust in my eyes.

"Shhh! Don't talk," she uttered in a low tone while climbing back into my lap. I squeezed both of her breasts with my hands, taking turns going back and forth sucking her nipples hungrily. "Ahhh, shit yes!" she cried out, sliding down my dick.

"Fuck, Paris!" I mumbled while working my way back to her soft lips.

I couldn't get enough of her pretty ass. Her pussy was so tight and dripping wet, which let me know that she had been keeping it tight for me. She was feeling so good that I was on the verge of nutting already.

"Slow down girl, you tryna make a nigga nut?"

"Oh my god, it feels good," she moaned, rocking back and forth on me. "UMMM YESSSSS! Just like that! FUCK ME!" she cried out as I slammed in and out of her from underneath.

"You about to cum, ain't you?"

'Yes, baby, I'm about to cum!"

"Let that shit go! Cum on your dick," I commanded, feeling my nuts tightening up. I picked her up and walked over to the railing on the deck slamming her up and down on my dick until her legs started to tremble. "There you go, pretty."

"Ahhh, baby I'm cumming, I'm cumming I'm cumming! Yesssssss, yesssssss!" she yelled, throwing her head back, holding on to me for dear life.

"Ah shit, I'm cumming witcha!" I moaned, pounding her insides nonstop, releasing deep inside of her. After I gained control of myself, I walked backwards collapsing on the chair.

"That was intense," she panted breathlessly, laying her head on my chest.

"That was everything, P. After the day I just had, that was exactly what a nigga needed," I admitted, wrapping my arms around her body that was trembling. "Are you cold? We can go inside."

"No, I'm fine. Just hold me, and don't let me go," she expressed, looking up pecking my lips.

"I got you, Paris."

For the next thirty minutes, we sat outside enjoying the night air watching the view of the ocean. I realized Paris had drifted off to sleep by the time I was ready to go inside. I carried her upstairs, laid her on my bed, and then went to run a hot bath for us. After the Jacuzzi tub filled up, I came back in the room to get her. Picking her up off the bed, I kissed her lips repeatedly until she woke up.

"Paris, wake up baby."

"I'm tired, Jinx," she whined, laying her head on my chest.

"You made all that food for a nigga don't you want me to eat it?"

"Yes. I guess I'll wake up." When we got to the bathroom, I put Paris down then got in the tub. After I was comfortable, I helped her get in. "Oh my god, this water feels so good Jinx."

"I know, right. I don't get in here often because I'm really too tall for this tub, but tonight I'll make an exception for you.

"I'm sure you paid a lot of money for this house, why don't you just get another tub put in here."

"I've been thinking about it, but haven't got around to doing it. So what's up? What you been doing since you cut my ass off?" I teased, splashing water in her face. That's when I noticed her hair was different.

"I did not cut you off. I was just mad at you. Why are you looking at me like that?"

"What you do to your hair? I like it."

"I washed it. My hair is naturally curly. I just keep it straight most of the time."

"I like it like this."

"Thanks."

"You never answered my question. What have you been up to?"

"Same shit different day, working every day, coming home, and getting up the next day to do it all over again. One thing I did accomplish was I think I found a spot for the boys and girls club I was telling you that I wanted to open."

"Really? That's what's up. Where is it located?"

"It's in Gardena, but it's the perfect location, near Rosecrans and Van Ness. So many abandoned buildings are for sale. My bestie showed me a few properties when we were out shopping a few weeks ago. It's in a neutral area where there isn't a lot of gang activity."

"I keep forgetting Dream's a realtor. So you're serious about opening a community center?"

"Very serious. I saved up money for a whole year dancing to be able to get everything up and running. I plan to move forward with my vision."

"That's dope as fuck. I've been looking for something to invest in. What do you think about letting me help you? I have a few connects with contractors that will come out to take a look around for you."

"That's the only thing stopping me now is figuring out who to trust with my vision. There are so many shady contractors that I wouldn't know where to start. I would love for you to help me take on this project. That will give us more time to spend together."

"I'm wit it."

"You're actually going to be a big help to me. You come from the streets, so you know exactly what it is these kids need in a center like I want to open."

"I got you with whatever you need. Just let me know. When you get some time, I want to go check this place out."

"I'm excited." She smiled, clapping her hands together."

"You are silly as hell."

"I know," she teased. "What have you been up to since the last time we saw each other?" she asked, rubbing her feet up and down my chest under the water.

"Man, besides calling yo ass, getting sent to voicemail, I've been doing what I do best— chasing paper and chilling with the gang."

"It feels like I see Gunna every day now. My sister loves his rude ass." Paris smiled, shaking her head."

"You probably do. That lovesick nigga is not gone let yo sister be out of his sight for too long."

"You right about that." She laughed. "Did you know White Boy and Dream have been kicking it lately?"

"Nah, he didn't tell me," I lied, taking her foot bringing it to my mouth placing light kisses up her leg, working my way back down to her feet. "I love your pretty ass toes."

"Ummm don't start nothing you don't have time to finish," she moaned as I massaged her foot.

"I got all night."

"No, you don't. We are about to get out this tub and go downstairs so I can make your plate."

"So, I can't have no more pussy first?"

"Nope. Come on, let's go take a shower then go downstairs so you can eat this food."

"You're ruining the mood."

"No, I'm not. You're just trying to get some more pussy."

"What's wrong with that," I laughed, helping her out of the tub.

"There's nothing wrong, that can wait till later. Remember you said we had all night," she smirked, stepping back so that I could cut the water on in the shower. Once the water was hot, we both got in, washed up, and then got out going back to my bedroom.

*

"Paris, that food was good as fuck!" I leaned back at the table, rubbing my stomach.

"Thank you. I'm glad you liked it."

"That shit hit the spot. I'm nice and full now, ready to lay it out."

"No Jinx. We haven't seen each other in over a month, and you said we were going to make up for lost time."

"My bad, you're right. Walk outside with me to get my weed out the car."

"It's after one in the morning. Is it necessary to get high right now?"

"It's never too late to smoke some bomb ass weed. Are you coming or not?"

"Of course, I'm coming. Let me get my sweater first."

"You don't need it. I'll keep yo pretty ass warm," I smirked, standing up wrapping my arms around her. "Come on, let's go."

When we got to the front door, I asked Paris to close her eyes. Thinking I was just being silly, she went ahead and played along.

"Open your eyes, Paris."

"Oh my god Jinx, you didn't!"

"I did, do you like it?" I asked as she ran around her new G-Wagon, jumping up and down. "Hell yeah, I like it. Matter of fact I love my new car. Look at these rims and this paint job!"

"I'm glad you like it. This is a part of my apology for Shaneka messing up your car."

"Thank you, bae!"

Paris ran over to me jumping in my arms while kissing me all over my face. She couldn't believe I bought her a new G-Wagon to replace her old one when only the windows needed to be replaced. Paris's new truck was all black, with dark tinted windows and twenty-four-inch custom rims.

"You're welcome, Paris. Come check out the inside." My mouth hit the floor when I opened the driver's side door. The black leather interior and Sony sound system had to cost a pretty penny. "Damn P, this wagon fits you perfectly."

"I think I'll call her the black widow." She laughed, getting out of the car."

"Can I get some pussy now?"

"Not yet. Go get the keys. I want to take this baby for a quick spin."

"You know what, fuck it. I'll be right back," I said, walking off to get the keys.

Chapter Twenty-Two

LUNDYN

I waited on a new client to arrive at the hair salon bright and early this morning. I always try to make a good impression when I'm conducting business. However, my client was running thirty minutes late and hadn't called or even texted to say she would be late, which I hated with a passion. If you cannot make it or show up a few minutes late, then that's fine with me because either way, I already got the deposit for half of my services up front.

I decided to send Gunna a quick text while I waited.

Me: *Morning, baby, you still sleeping?*

Gunna: *Nah, I'm up about to go make my rounds. You done with your first appointment?*

Me: *No, the bitch is running late.*

Gunna: *Fuck her. Come back to my house and get in bed.*

Me: *I can't. I have three heads this morning. Can you bring me some food?*

Gunna: *You gone let me fuck?*

Me: *Never mind, you're so nasty. Can you ever be serious?*

Gunna: *Shit, I am serious.*

Me: *Bye, I'll text Rasheed* 😒

When he didn't bother to respond, I knew I had pissed him off. As soon as I picked up my purse and car keys to get food, my new client came strolling in.

"Hey, Lundyn, right?"

"Are you Nikki?"

"Yes, that's me. You look different on Instagram," she smirked, rubbing me the wrong way. "You do know your appointment was an hour ago, right?"

"Girl, my bad, I overslept, I'm here now though, so let's get started." She shrugged, brushing me off.

"Let's be clear, Nikki. I'm charging you an extra fifty dollars for wasting my time and being late. And for future reference, if you show up this late again, then I will cancel your appointment. Is that understood?"

"I don't like your attitude, but I hear you.

"I don't like the way your eyebrows are connecting, but then again that's probably why you're here now."

"I'm only getting my hair weaved!" she spat, turning her lip up at me.

"No, Nikki, I insist. I'll fix your eyebrows for you free of charge." I laughed under my breath. This hoe thought she was funny, but I had jokes for days. I washed and blow-dried Nikki's hair without saying another word to her.

When I sent her to sit under the dryer the door to my private suite opened, and Gunna walked in looking pissed, carrying a bag from Tams.

"What was that hot shit you were spitting over the phone?" he snapped, walking up on me.

"I was just playing, and I have a client under the dryer, so don't start."

"You know better than playing with me like that. Fuck is your problem?"

"I'm hungry."

"And I'm horny, so you need to take care of your nigga."

"I have a client what do you want me to do?"

"Where she at?"

"Back there under the dryer."

"Let's go to my truck. All I need is ten minutes."

"Hell no!"

"Let's go in the bathroom then, Lundyn," he suggested, pulling me off to my personal bathroom. Nikki was scrolling on her phone, so I went ahead and let him have his way. "Take your shorts off."

"Baby, I'm not about to get naked in this bathroom," I expressed, as he picked me up placing me on the sink. He pushed me backwards and unfastened my jean shorts while pulling them down over my ass. After pushing my thong to the side, he dove in head first sucking on my clit just how I liked.

"Ummm, baby!"

Pulling my thong completely off he stuffed it in my mouth, before going back to feast on my goodies. I was spent after two orgasms, but he was just getting started. There was a chair in my bathroom, so he carried me over to it laying me back while twisting my body up like a pretzel.

"I know you gotta get back to work, so I'm about to murder this pussy Savage Boyz style," he smirked while pushing his way inside of me.

"Shit, baby slow down!"

"Nah, Lun, take this dick. Next time you threaten me with another nigga I'ma fuck you up!"

"I'm sorry baby! Ahh, yess beat this pussy up!" What was supposed to be a ten-minute session turned into thirty. After my fifth orgasm, Gunna finally came right behind me. We both were out of breath ready for a nap after that intense sex.

Knock! Knock!

"Hello! Lundyn, are you in there?" Nikki banged on the door.

"I'm coming out right now."

"She probably heard us," Gunna laughed, standing to his feet. I took the walk of shame out of the bathroom after cleaning up as best as I could.

"Gunna?" Nikki smirked, when he walked out after me.

"Wait, how do y'all know each other babe?" I inquired, turning to Gunna.

"I used to let her suck me off." He shrugged.

"Used too, ha! That's funny." Nikki tossed her head back, laughing. However, I didn't find shit funny.

"So you saying you sucked his dick recently?"

"That's your bae, why don't you ask him," Nikki smirked, looking at Gunna.

"Bitch, don't play with me! I ain't let you suck me off in months. Fuck is wrong with yo dumb ass!" he hissed through clenched teeth.

"Was I a bitch when you let me suck your dick two weeks ago at the strip club?"

"Bitch, you a muthafuckin' lie! You begged me to suck my dick, and I told you I was good. Don't ever lie on my dick, hoe!"

"Nikki, get the fuck out! I now see your motive for coming to see me was to get under my skin."

"What about my hair?"

"What about it? I have the right to refuse service to anyone I choose. Now get the fuck out!"

"Bitch, you about to finish my hair! This is bad business!"

"Losing you as a customer won't hurt my pockets, and you can say whatever you want about me when you leave here because my work speaks for itself. Now get out before I drag your ass the fuck out!"

"It's cool. I'll just take my money up the block to Tay's salon U Pay I Slay. Her work is better than yours, anyway!"

"That's my girl so no offense taken over here. Tay is a beast at what she does. Tell her I said what's up when you get there. Matter of fact I'ma call her and let her know not to fuck with your baldheaded ass. She only deals with healthy hair, and that's not your type boo. Bye!"

"Put me out?"

"It will be my pleasure," I smiled deviously, walking over to her purse. I picked it up along with her cheap ass Ali Express bundles and tossed it out the back door of my suite.

"You got me fucked up hoe!" She hopped up trying to swing on me, but I dropped her ass with a quick two-piece then dragged her out the door by the little hair she had on her head.

"Pussy ass hoe, don't ever try me again!"

"Let her ass know, Lundyn!" Gunna laughed, trying to hype me up, but his stupid ass was next.

"Gunna, you can get the fuck out right along with this hoe!"

"What the fuck I do? Why you mad at me?"

"You should have mentioned it to me the day that bitch tried to suck your dick, but you didn't. So in my eyes, either your lying or you got something to hide."

"Lundyn, are you serious right now?"

"Why are you still here? Get the fuck out! If I can't trust you, then we don't need to be together. I'm good on you, nigga. It's over!"

"You can't be serious right now! I love the fuck out of you, and it's gone take a lot more than that to get me to leave. Fuck what you talking about. I'm not going no fucking where!"

"You know what? I'll leave. My next appointment isn't until twelve, so that gives me more than enough free time to be on my good bullshit!"

Getting my keys, I unlocked the drawer that I kept my purse in then walked out the back door. Gunna was right behind me when I got to my car.

"Lundyn! Are you really gone believe that bitch over me? I told you we didn't do shit, she lying!"

"You should have told me when it first happened. I don't believe you. I told you not to play with me, but I guess you have to learn the hard way."

"I love you, bae. You should already know that. I've changed a lot of my ways all because I didn't want to hurt you, and you still believe the next bitch over me."

"I gotta go. Maybe I'll see you around."

Unlocking my car, I slid inside then peeled out of the parking lot in tears. I may have been overreacting, but I had to prove a point. Never leave your woman in a position where another bitch can make her look like a fool. If it was really nothing to the story, then Gunna could have come to me when it happened. That way if it were ever brought to me, I would already know what was up. Pulling up to my house, I hopped out the car and went straight to the kitchen to make me something to eat.

I made four pieces of French toast, scrambled eggs, fresh strawberries, and turkey sausage then washed it down with a big glass of orange juice. As I was eating, I heard the front door open and close. Paris walked in the kitchen seconds later.

"Morning Lun, what are you doing here? I thought you would be at the shop today?"

"Hey, sis, I was at the shop. I came back home till my next appointment at noon."

"What's wrong?"

"I don't want to talk about it right now."

"Are you sure?"

"I'm positive, Paris."

"Alright, did you make enough food for me? I'm starving."

"There's a piece of French toast left and a couple of pieces of sausage in the pan on the stove."

"I know you didn't eat a whole pack of turkey sausage by yourself, Lundyn."

"I was starving. I've been eating everything in sight lately."

"Maybe it's from stress, are you sure you're alright?"

"Yeah, I promise it's nothing I can't handle. I just fought with Gunna earlier. Where are you coming from?"

"Jinx wanted to see the location for the community center that I'm about to open not too far from here. He wants to invest in it."

"That's what's up, sis. Let me know if you need my help with anything."

"I have a few ideas in mind already, but I'll run it back pass you once I get everything together. Right now, my focus is on securing the property."

"Aww Paris, I'm so proud of you."

"Thanks, Lun. That means a lot to me."

"I haven't seen you in almost a week, so I guess it's safe to say things went well between you and Jinx."

"Yeah, things have been perfect between us. We back like we never left."

While she was talking, a wave of nausea hit me. I took off running to the bathroom, throwing up everything I just ate. As I dry heaved over the toilet, Paris came behind me holding my hair.

"Lundyn, that's what you get for eating all that food greedy," she teased.

"I don't feel good, Paris," I cried as I continued vomiting. Once I got it all out, I brushed my teeth then dragged myself into the shower. I felt so bad that I could barely wash myself up, so I rinsed off then went to my room to lie down.

"Paris!"

"What's up, Lundyn? You feel any better?"

"Not at all, I feel so weak. Can you please call the salon and tell them to call and cancel the rest of my appointments for the day?"

"I got you boo. Lie down and get you some rest. Maybe those eggs were bad."

"I promise never to eat another egg."

"You're so damn silly. Get some rest. I'll be back to check on you in a little bit."

"Alright, sis, thanks."

Chapter Twenty-Three

GUNNA

Lundyn had me so mad when she left her shop today that I was in a fucked up mood for the rest of the day. After I made my rounds checking on the weed dispensaries and traps, I took my black ass home. Lundyn obviously didn't know what type of hold she really has on me, and that's crazy. For her to let another bitch put some bullshit in her ear and actually believe her over me, was foul as fuck. Before Lundyn, I didn't give bitches the time of day. There wasn't a female alive besides her I ever fucked with on this level. I'm used to busting one off in a hoe mouth, and then I'd send her on about her day.

Tired of sitting at home mad cause Lundyn wasn't answering any of my calls, so I hit up my niggas who convinced me to go out with them. We ended up at V Live L.A., which will be my last time coming to this low budget ass strip club. Looking at these tired ass hoes had me ready to go lay up with my girl. After I guzzled down my glass of Henny, a crazy thought came to mind.

"Aye Jinx, I need you to ride out with me real quick." I stood up to leave.

"Where we going?" he asked as we walked out the club to my Chevy Tahoe.

"Don't ask. You might try and talk me out of it."

"Ahh shit, nigga, don't do nothing crazy bro."

"Nigga, I am crazy," I laughed, passing him a Ziploc bag of Kush and some cigarillos. "Roll up!"

It took me about fifteen minutes to reach my destination in the City of Hawthorne. After passing two blunts back and forth, I checked to make sure my pistol was loaded then hopped out the car.

Ding Dong!

"Who is it?"

"Me, baby open up!" Seconds later, the door was opened as I pushed my way inside.

"Ahhhh!" Nikki screamed, backing away from me. "Wh... why do you have a gun pointed at me?" she asked with tears in her eyes.

"Shut the fuck up, bitch!" *Wham!* I slapped the fuck outta her stupid ass. "I don't even believe in hitting women, but you deserved that shit you lying bitch!"

"Gunna, I'm sorry! I don't know why I lied. I promise it won't ever happen again!"

"shut the fuck up bitch and let's go!"

"Wh-where are we going?"

"You ask too many fuckin' questions. Bring your ass on."

"Bro, walk it off! I'll bring her to the truck," Jinx shook his head.

I felt myself getting angrier by the second, so I walked off before I snapped Nikki's fuckin' neck. Minutes later, Jinx walked out of the house with Nikki walking closely in front of him. Once they made it to the truck, I hopped out and popped the trunk.

"You're tripping, G. It's too many eyes to put this bitch in the trunk. Hogtie her ass and toss her in the backseat.

I wasn't prepared, so I passed him the keys to my truck so he could drive, and I got in the backseat. Nikki was shaking like a stripper, but I didn't give a fuck. Next time she will know not to fuck with what's mine.

"You know where we headed?"

"Yeah, G." Jinx shook his head as he pulled off. It took us no time to get to Gardena.

"I'll be right back. If she makes a sound, kill her dumb ass."

"Hurry up. I got shit to do."

I knocked on the front door for ten minutes before Lundyn answered with her hair all over her head.

"Lundyn, what's wrong?"

"Gunna, why are you here this time of night? Have you been drinking?"

"Yeah, my niggas and me went out tonight."

"Look, I don't feel good, and I told you that I was cool on you. Why are you here?"

"Come outside. Let me show you something."

"Gunna, no, it's cold, now bye."

"Man, bring yo ass on!" Stepping into some slippers by the door, she hesitantly walked outside with me.

"What are you up to now, Gunna?"

"You're about to see right now, sit tight." Pulling the back door open, Nikki's eyes got wide as saucers.

"Gunna, really?" Lundyn spat, smacking me in the back of my head. "Why is this bitch here?" Ignoring Lundyn's question, I grabbed Nikki by her weave, pulling her to me, while holding my pistol under her chin.

"Nikki, did we fuck at the strip club ever?"

"N-nnn-nooo I..I li...lied!" she stuttered, stumbling over her words.

"When the last time I let you suck my dick?"

"Itttt...was ... mmmonths ago," Nikki cried, trembling in fear.

"Why the fuck did you lie to my girl?"

"Be ...because I mmiisss you," she confessed. "I'm sorry, please let me go."

"Ima let you go, but if you go to the police or tell anyone what happened tonight. Your parents who live on and 54th and Denker are gone come up missing!"

"No, please, that's not necessary! You have my word. I won't go to the police. Please just let me go."

"Now get the fuck out."

"How am I supposed to get home?"

"You better beat your fucking feet like Fred Flintstone. Now go!" Nikki took off running down the street as if her ass was on fire.

"Gunna, you have lost your damn mind?" Lundyn snapped getting in my face. "I can't believe you just did that. Why would you come where I lay my head with this bullshit! Jinx, you wait till I tell Paris your stupid ass drove him over here too. I can't believe y'all! I'm still not fuckin' with you Gunna. You may have not let that girl suck your dick, but the fact remains you've been keeping secrets from me. I would never lie to you, no matter what. Just like I'm woman enough to tell you that I've been on the phone with Rasheed half of the day when I was ignoring your calls," Lundyn smirked.

Bam! Bam! Bam!

She jumped back after I put my fist through my passenger and back window, cutting my hand up in the process. She broke down to the ground crying, but I had no more words for her.

Opening the passenger door, I hopped back in my truck, and Jinx pulled off, leaving Lundyn right where she was. *Fuck her!*

Chapter Twenty-Four

JINX

For two weeks, I've been in the doghouse after pulling that stunt with Gunna's crazy ass. He was my bro, so when he asked me to roll with him, I didn't ask any questions, I just went. Although I wasn't gone let him kill Nikki's dumb ass, I still should have handled that situation differently. Paris was livid after finding out that I was involved and put my ass on the block list for almost a week before she calmed down.

After talking to Dream a few days ago, I learned that Paris was approved for the building she purchased for the community center. I had a few connects with contractors and electricians, so I hit them up and started the process of getting the building up to code for the inspectors. After picking Paris up from work this afternoon, I was on my way to surprise her with the good news hoping that would get me back in her good graces.

Pulling up to the building where the community center will be located, I had Paris blindfolded as I helped her out of the car.

"Jinx where are we? I'm so nervous."

"Don't be. I promise you're going to be excited."

"I can't wait to see what you have up your sleeve, babe."

"Watch your step." When we made it to the front entrance, I

removed her blindfold while putting the keys to the building in her hands. "Open your eyes, P."

"Oh my god! Does this mean I got approved?" she asked, jumping up and down.

"That's exactly what it means. Dream told me a few days ago. I made her promise not to tell you. Come on, let's go inside."

"Oh my god, Jinx, is this really happening? Wait, has someone been working in here?"

"Yes. I hired a few people to bring the building up to code. After you finish your paperwork, you can probably have the building inspector come out within the next two or three weeks."

"I can't believe you did all this for me. Thank you so much, babe," she cried, wrapping her arms around my waist.

"Why the fuck are you crying, Paris. I thought you would be happy."

"I am happy, Jinx. You just don't understand how long I've wanted to do this, and it's finally happening. I danced all last year to save up money for this. I'm so excited."

"As you should be. You made so many sacrifices for your family, Paris. If nobody ever told you, I want you to know that I'm proud of you."

"Thank you so much, babe."

"You're welcome. I got you every step of the way. Now all you need to do is think of a name for the community center, and tell me what you need me to pay for so that I can cut you a check."

"I haven't even thought of what colors I want or anything. Thanks again."

"We can sit down and look over some ideas whenever you have time."

"That sounds like a good idea."

"So does this mean you're not mad at me no more?" I smiled, leaning down to kiss her pretty ass.

"I haven't been mad at you ever since I unblocked you from calling me." She smiled, staring up at me.

"So, does this mean I can have some pussy? I need to bust a nut."

"After you take me to dinner and a movie, I promise to take care of you, babe." She laughed, backing away from me.

"It's dinner time now, so where you tryna go?"

"It doesn't matter, as long as we're together."

"Aight bet. Come on, let's go."

After eating dinner at Crustacean's, Paris greedy ass said fuck the movies and decided just to go back to her house to Netflix and chill. I didn't object because I already knew what time it was. We pulled up to the house the same time as Lundyn.

"Where is your sister coming from this time of night?"

"Probably the salon. It's Friday, so one of her clients probably had a late appointment."

"Yeah aight, let me find out you covering for your sister. Ain't nobody getting they hair done this time of night."

"Jinx, it's just 10:30. I've been in the salon way later than this before."

"I'm still about to text my bro and tell him to come check on his girl."

"Please don't. Lundyn has been cool on him ever since y'all stupid ass came here and scared her half to death."

"That was her fault." I shrugged. "Didn't nobody tell her to say that dumb shit she said to my bro. Gunna is real life 51/50. He's calmed down so much since he been kicking it with your sister. I can honestly say he been on the straight and narrow ever since they linked back up."

"Well, hopefully, she will come around eventually."

"Here she comes now. I thought she went into the house. I wonder what happened."

"We about to find out."

Knock! Knock!

Rolling the driver's side window down, I could tell that something was wrong.

"Jinx, when I made it to the front door, it was open. I forgot my gun in the house, so I'm not going inside."

"I'll check it out, but you need to call your nigga."

"That's not my man, but I did already. He said he's five minutes away."

"Jinx, please wait on him to get here," Paris voiced nervously.

"I ain't scared to go in alone. What the fuck is you saying?"

"I'm not saying you're scared. Just don't walk into a trap trying to be brave, Jinx!" Seconds later, I heard tires screech. Looking out my rearview, Gunna hopped out the car walking over to Lundyn.

Chapter Twenty-Five

LUNDYN

"What the fuck is going on, Lun?" Gunna asked, checking me for marks like I had been hurt.

"Gunna, I don't know. When I got to the front door, it was slightly open. I didn't bother going inside because I didn't have my pistol on me. Since Jinx was sitting here, I came and told him what was going on after I called you."

"Get in the car with Paris until we come back out to get you."

"Are you sure, Gunna?"

"Baby, I'm positive."

Jinx hopped out the car, and I sat in the driver's seat, waiting on them to return.

"Paris, are you sure you locked the door when you left?"

"I'm positive. I wonder why I didn't get an alert on my phone if someone broke in."

"Paris, I don't know, but I pray this is nothing. Why would someone want to break in now after we've been living here all this time with no issue?"

"Here they come now. Let's just see what happened."

"Go get in my car, Lundyn. Y'all can't stay here tonight," Gunna insisted, after opening the door.

"What's going on?"

"Y'all house is trashed. Somebody broke in and destroyed everything. Even y'all clothes were torn to shreds!"

"What! Please tell me you're playing?"

"Nah Lun, I'm dead ass serious."

"We can't just leave. I have to call the police to make a report. We have insurance that will cover any damages made to the house!" Paris voiced.

"The house is fucked. We just checked, and there's no one inside, so you can come see for yourself Paris," Gunna explained.

"Oh my god, the house! Paris, look at this shit!" I screamed in disbelief.

"What the fuck? Who would do this to us?" Paris yelled with tears in her eyes.

"Nah, fuck that, Gunna. This probably had something to do with your little bitch Nikki!" I snapped, mushing him in the face.

"This ain't got shit to do with me! Nikki knows exactly how I get down. She knows better. Just like you need to know if you put yo fuckin' hands on me again, I'm fucking you up."

"If that hood rat bitch knew better, then she wouldn't have been running her mouth at the salon. Look at this house. It's trashed!"

"I already handled Nikki!" Gunna hissed, running his hands over his waves.

"Sis, please calm down. This material shit can be replaced. All I keep thinking about is what could have happened if one of us was home when this shit went down. I didn't get any alerts from the security company. This shit is unbelievable," Paris rambled on while looking through her iPhone.

"This is most definitely personal. Whoever did this knew what they were doing," Jinx explained, looking around the house. "Go check y'all bedrooms and see if anything is missing or if they just destroyed everything."

"Yeah, let's go check, Paris."

As I walked through the house, I shook my head, looking at how someone had destroyed all the hard work Paris had done turning this house into our home over the years. I cut the light on when I walked

into my room and immediately wanted to turn around and walk back
out. My room was in shambles, but my bed was still intact. Even all of
my little trinkets were still on the dresser. However, entering my huge
walk-in closet, the first thing I did was check on my jewelry in the safe.
Every single item was still there. *That's strange.* Turning around to see
every piece of clothing I owned torn to shreds had me in my feelings
immediately. All of my things and designer bags were ruined. I cut the
light, not wanting to see anymore and walked out.

"Ahhh, oh my god!" I heard Paris scream.

When I made it to her room, I couldn't believe my eyes. It was as if
someone had literally taken a sledgehammer and busted her TV,
mirrors, and even her bed was destroyed. All the clothes in her closet
were torn to shreds just like mine. Even her shoes were damaged, and
she had hundreds of shoes.

"The wires from the alarm system were cut. That's why you weren't
notified Paris," Gunna explained, shaking his head after walking in her
bedroom.

"Paris, what are we going to do? We can't stay here. I don't feel safe
anymore."

"What about your room, how bad was the damage?"

"My room isn't as bad as yours, but there's still thousands of dollars'
worth of damage.

"Are you serious?"

"Yes."

"So this was a personal attack on me, this is crazy."

"I don't know P. Who have you pissed off?"

"No one, I have no enemies, Lundyn." Paris sighed in frustration.

"Do you think dad had something to do with this?"

"Now that you mention it, he could have something to do with
this. I'm definitely gone have to visit his punk ass!"

"You already know I got your back sis, just say the word. Let's get
this house cleaned up, and then we can figure out our next move. I'm
so sorry all of your things were destroyed. Whatever you need that I
have, it's yours," I cried, wrapping my arms around Paris who stood
crying silently.

"Y'all just stay calm and let me and Jinx handle this shit. I just called for help, we will have this place cleaned up in no time," Gunna reassured us.

"Thanks you guys, but I have to take pictures of the damage and file a police report first. I told you, I have insurance that will cover all the damages and replace all the material things we lost. This is an inconvenience, but a blessing in disguise. After the insurance company cuts me a check, I will have a brand new wardrobe, fully furnished house, and new jewelry to replace what they stole." Paris smiled, wiping at her tear stained face.

"Well, I think I did have a few very expensive items missing out of my room now that I think about it," I teased, lying through my teeth, making everyone laugh.

"Gunna, let's go wait outside while they call twelve. I don't want to be nowhere around them muthafuckas."

"Facts— you don't gotta tell me twice. I'm right behind you, bro," Gunna added. "Lundyn, I'll be outside until twelve come and leave. We need to talk, so I'll holla at you in a minute."

"Yeah, ok." I rolled my eyes before walking off.

❧

An hour later, the police had come out to make a report, assess the damages, and then left after leaving their card behind.

"Paris, what are we going to do sis?" I inquired, walking in the kitchen where she was sitting in the only non-broken chair.

"I just reserved us a two-bedroom suite at the Embassy Suites near LAX. You can leave and go there now, or you can stay here and wait on me. It's up to you."

"Why are you staying here?"

"I have to wait on these people to board up the two windows that were broken."

"Paris, you should already know I'm not leaving without you. You get on my nerves, but you know you my bestie," I teased.

"Girl whatever, I need a drink."

"There's plenty of liquor in the refrigerator. I guess the robbers didn't want no alcohol." I smiled, trying to lighten the mood.

"Well, please pour us a drink. What a day. It started perfect up until this point."

"We gone get through this just like everything else, together."

"Thanks, sister."

"You're welcome, boo."

"Lundyn, let me holla at you real quick!" Gunna snapped, walking in the kitchen.

"Don't you see we're having a sister moment?"

"You really have been testing my patience lately, Lundyn. The only reason I let you get away with it this long is because I fucked up."

"Ugh!" I rolled my eyes being petty. "Paris, I'll be back. Let me go see what this fool wants!" I spat, walking out of the kitchen. I made sure I took my time walking slowly to my bedroom because I knew Gunna was on his good bullshit.

"Yeah, ok. I want you to keep this same energy when we get inside the room."

"What's that supposed to mean?"

"Get yo ass in the bedroom. I don't got all night."

Opening my bedroom door, I walked inside, slamming it in Gunna's face. I laughed all the way to the bed before sitting down and crossing my legs. After about five minutes went by, Gunna still hadn't walked in the room. Just before I got up to see where he was, the door opened. He walked in my bedroom smoking a fat ass blunt. He gave me a menacing glare then closed the door, locking it behind him.

"Lundyn, come here," he uttered in a tone so cold that it sent chills down my spine. I nervously walked over to him.

"What's up, bae?" He turned his head to the side staring into my eyes. "Bae, what's wrong?"

"Take this shit off."

"What? I'm not fuckin' you. You better call Nikki."

"By the time I finish this blunt, you better be ass naked." The cocky smirk on his face had my clit throbbing. By the time he finished his blunt, I was ass naked pussy dripping wet. "Go lie on the bed and play with that pretty ass pussy."

"Are you serious, Gunna?"

"Come here."

I slowly walked over to him. He grabbed me by my ponytail then pulled me in for a kiss that made my knees buckle.

"Ummmm," I moaned as he bit down on my bottom lip. He took his hand and moved it between my legs, playing in my wetness and used his thumb to circle my clit applying just the right amount of pressure. "Damn, this feels good."

"Go lay down," he demanded, removing his hand. Walking over to the bed, I laid down, took my left hand then started playing in my wetness, completely turned on. "There you go. You so fucking beautiful, Lundyn." I kept my eyes on him as I felt a powerful orgasm approaching.

"You been giving my pussy away?" he asked, watching me pleasure myself.

"N...no never, Gunna."

"You better not have. Go ahead and let that shit go. Cum for me, Lundyn." As soon as the words left his mouth, a powerful orgasm hit me full force.

"Ughhhh yessss ...I'm cumming!"

He climbed on top of me, kissing my lips like he craved everything about them. Grabbing my hand, he took my fingers and licked every trace of my sweet essence off each one of them. "Gunna, baby, I'm sorry for being a bitch."

"Nah keep that same energy you had earlier Lun," he smirked, rising off me. My mouth watered watching him remove his clothes one piece at a time. "Fuck is yo ass looking at? Come here."

Crawling over to him, I got off the bed standing to my feet.

"What's up? I asked as he led me over to the chair that was barely standing in the corner of my room. My body began to shiver from nervousness.

"Bend over, put both of your hands behind your back, and you better not fuckin' move."

"W-what I'm gone fall. This ch-chair is broken," I stuttered.

"Don't make me repeat myself." Doing as I was told, I bent over the chair placing both of my hands behind my back, crisscrossing them at the wrist. *Smack! Smack!*

"Awww, shit!" I cried out.

Moments later, Gunna dived in head first eating my pussy from behind. He had every single nerve ending in my body on fire as he took my body to new heights of pleasure. I started to tremble as he slid his tongue in and out of my slippery opening. "Oh my goodness baby, yessss. Please don't stop, right their baby!" *Smack!*

"Is this what yo ass needed? You needed daddy to suck on that pussy?" *Smack!* "You don't hear me talking to you, Lundyn Monroe? Answer me!"

"Y...yeeee-yes, baby! This is exactly what I needed. I'm about to cum again! Fuck, I'm about to cum! Gunnaaa, please don't stop!"

"Nah fuck that, you hurt a nigga feelings dumping me and shit. You need to apologize." he laughed, standing to his feet backing away from me. I turned my head around so fast that I felt my neck snap.

"Get back over here? What are you doing? I was about to cum!"

He sat on the bed laughing, but I was about to bite his ass. Now was not the time to be playing with me. It has been two weeks since we last had sex, and I was long overdue. Getting up off the chair, walking over to him, I pushed him down on his back and straddled his lap.

"You not about to come over here and fuck the shit out of me. Watch out, Lun!" He picked me up flipping me around placing me on my back while he hovered over me. "Why did I have to bring Nikki over here at gunpoint for you to believe I didn't let her suck my dick?"

"Are you fucking serious right now, Gunna?" I asked while grinding my hips in a circular motion."

"Dead ass serious. Now answer my question and stop popping yo pussy like you one of the damn City Girls! You gone get this dick whenever I give it to you."

"Finish eating my pussy Gunna. I'm horny."

"Why didn't you believe me?" Wrapping his hand around his dick, he tapped it lightly on my clit, driving me insane. "Damn, you wet ass fuck!" With just the tip, he pushed in and out of my slippery opening. "Since you're not answering my question, I guess that means you don't want no dick."

Waiting for him to push back inside of me, I raised my hips causing him to slip inside filling me up completely. "Fuck! He quickly pulled out and then started sucking on my clit. Right when I was getting ready to cum again, he stopped.

"Oh my god, please stop torturing me!" I whined, ready to pull my hair out. "I always believed you Gunna. I just didn't like the fact you were hiding shit from me!"

"Were you really talking to Rasheed?"

"No! I just wanted you to hurt like I was hurt. I'm sorry ok, now put it back in!"

"Why didn't you say that ten minutes ago?"

"Put it in!" I snapped through gritted teeth.

"Get on top. If you want this dick as bad as I think you do, come get this muthafucka," he urged, teasing me with the tip of his dick again.

"Fuck this!" I screamed in frustration.

Using all my strength, I pushed him off me. Standing to my feet, I pushed him backwards on the bed then straddled his lap. He had a sexy smirk on his face looking into my eyes as I slid down on his erection.

Ahhhhh!" I cried out, not moving a muscle enjoying the feeling of him being deep inside of me.

"Get that dick. Let me see you work this tight ass pussy." *Smack*!

That was all the motivation I needed. Interlocking his fingers with mine, I took him on a ride he will never forget.

"Fuck, Lun!" he moaned as I rocked back and forth on him.

I rode him so good working my hips that his mouth was hanging wide open. As I felt my orgasm approaching, I started going harder, raising up riding just the tip. When I felt his dick begin to jump, I knew he was about to come, so I slammed all the way down on him.

"Umm, fuck! Raise up I'm about to nut, Lundyn."

"Baby nooo.... I'm coming too! I love you! I love you so much, Gunna!" I cried out when I felt his load shoot deep inside of me. I came again right behind him with tears running down my face. "Oh my god, I love you, baby. I don't ever want to fight with you again," I mumbled, looking down at Gunna who was staring up at me with an expression that I couldn't read. "Baby, what's wrong?"

"Do you mean it?"

"Do I mean what?"

"Never mind watch out," he said, trying to push me off him.

"No, baby, wait! Tell me what you're talking about. Do I mean what?"

"You said you love me. Is it true?"

"Actually, yeah it is true. I've wanted to tell you for a minute, but I guess I've been too scared thinking that you would reject me."

"I love you too. I don't use that word loosely, so believe me when I say I love you."

I kissed his lips repeatedly as the tears began to freely fall down my face. I didn't even realize what I was saying in the heat of the moment, but I was glad he felt the same way I did.

"Gunna, we probably should go back in there with my sister and Jinx. We're not staying here tonight."

"Yeah, you're right we should, but man that nut got me ready to call it a night on the real." He laughed.

"I know, but we gotta get up. I'll be right back. Why don't you take a quick nap while I hop in the shower? By the time I got out and found the few pieces of clothing that were wearable, Gunna was already lightly snoring.

"Y'all don't care who knows y'all fuckin'. We done been robbed, the house is destroyed and y'all in the back fucking. Where they do that at?" Paris snapped while shaking her head.

Gunna and I looked at each other then fell out laughing because she was telling the truth. I can't blame her for being irritated. However, there was no shame in my game.

"My bad sister, you're right, but that was the best sex I've ever had."

"Yesirrrr!" Gunna agreed, wrapping his arms around my waist. "Ain't nothing better than makeup sex."

"I'm not even in the mood to go back and forth with y'all. Tonight has been full of craziness. Even though I made us hotel reservations, Jinx insists that I stay over his house tonight. Do you want to come with me?"

"Nah, she can stay the night with me at my house. It's not a problem," Gunna answered for me.

"Bae, are you sure?"

"Hell yeah, I'm sure," he replied.

"Well, it's only for tonight. Tomorrow, I'm checking into a hotel."

"The windows and the side door are boarded up until I can get them fixed. I'm ready to lay down. Can you please see if you have any nightclothes for me to sleep in. All of my things are ruined?" Paris asked, standing to her feet.

"Yeah, let me check. I still have a few things in my drawers that aren't ruined. That's where I got this from. What are you gonna do about work clothes next week?"

"I'm going to take next week off, just until I can get everything worked out with the insurance company. Oh yeah, before I forget, thank you both, Jinx and Gunna, for sending help to clean this mess up for us."

"You're welcome," they replied in unison.

"Paris, I'll go try and find you something to wear. Then we can get ready to leave."

"Alright, I'll be right here waiting for you.

Chapter Twenty-Six

PARIS

Buzz! Buzz!

Reaching underneath the pillow, I retrieved my phone that had been vibrating nonstop for the last ten minutes. After unlocking it, I sat up to check my notifications. I had Facebook messages, which I ignored, and a text message from an unsaved number.

Unknown: *Your time is up.*

After reading the text two more times, the wheels in my head started turning. I knew immediately that my father was behind the break-in at my house yesterday.

"Jinx! Baby, wake up!" I shook him until he stirred in his sleep.

"Paris, I'm sleep. What's up?" Wrapping his arms around my waist, he closed his eyes going back to sleep.

"Jinx, wake up! I think I know who was behind the break-in yesterday!" He jumped up, picking up his pistol off the nightstand.

"Who the fuck was it?"

"Read this." After reading over the text, he turned to me with a confused expression.

"Who the fuck is this?"

"I believe it's my father. Remember when I told you we got into it at our last visit?"

"Yeah, but you never really went into details."

"Well, he's mad because I refuse to meet up with an old business associate of his to pick up five keys of cocaine."

"What? When the fuck were you going to tell me any of this shit?"

"I didn't think he would actually make good on his threats. Since the visit, he's called threatening me a few times, but he's my father. I would never believe he would really send someone after me to hurt me."

"That's big Don-Don, not your father. When a muthafucka's back is against the wall, you will be surprised what a person will do. The first time he threatened you, you should have ran it pass me. That way I would've been on alert. I'm your man. It's my fucking job to protect you, Paris."

"Jinx, I'm sorry. I wasn't thinking."

"You're right. You weren't thinking. What else do I need to know?"

"I've told you everything. Over a month ago, he said I had seven days to meet up with Pablo. That time has come and gone, that's why I didn't take his threats seriously."

"Did you say, Pablo?"

"Yes. Pablo San Andreas. Do you know him?"

"I know exactly who you're talking about. That nigga got the heroin game on lock. After your pops got locked up, he took over his territory."

"Well, he owes my dad a favor. It looks like he may be fulfilling it by fucking with me.

"Let me hit up White Boy. That fool can get info on just about anyone in seconds."

"Ok. Let me call Lundyn and let her know what's going on."

After a few minutes of being on the phone, Jinx hung it up and gave me his full attention.

"White Boy said he would get back with me in thirty minutes or less. Did you talk to Lundyn?"

"Yes, she was on her way to the shop. She wants me to go get the room this morning while she's at work."

"Y'all don't need to be in no hotel right now Paris."

"I have to Jinx. I can't leave Lundyn alone by herself."

"Why doesn't she want to stay with her nigga?"

"I don't know, but I'll make sure I stay at the Marriot. They have extra security."

"I can't make you stay here, so I'll just come stay the night with you."

"That's fine with me. Lundyn just texted me and said she's leaving the shop at three to meet us at the Marriot near LAX so that we can check in our suite. Gunna will be with her, so you can come too if you want."

"I'll meet you there. I'm about to go make my rounds until we meet up."

"Go handle your business. I'll see you later, babe."

ॐ

After checking in our hotel, Jinx, Lundyn, Gunna and I rode the elevator back to the lobby after taking a few items upstairs. Stepping off the elevator, we headed towards the front exit. Lundyn and Gunna went their separate ways once we made it to the parking lot. Reaching into my purse, I pulled out my key fob. I then turned to Jinx and pulled him in for a hug while silently thanking God for him.

"I guess I'll talk to you later, Jinx."

"No, you will be seeing me later. Let's go to the beach."

"Oh, you trying to spend time with me?" I smiled, playfully hitting his arm.

"Of course, beautiful." He smiled. "You let a nigga hit in the bathroom just now, I think I need another shot. I'm hooked, Paris."

"Boy, you so crazy."

"Real shit P, I'm trying to get some more pussy tonight." He chuckled."

"Man, whatever. That's all you think about. Let's get out of here," I smiled, standing on my toes pecking his lips. "Can you walk me to my car?"

"Yeah, you know I got you." He wrapped his arms around my waist from behind while we walked towards my G-Wagon. When my car was in view, I pressed the button on my key fob twice to start the engine.

Boooooom!

The last thing I remember was feeling my body lift off the ground, throwing me almost fifty feet before I hit the ground with Jinx still behind me. We both went crashing to the ground with a loud thud as everything around me faded to darkness.

To Be Continued... The Finale drops later this month.

CPSIA information can be obtained
at www.ICGtesting.com
Printed in the USA
LVHW051550020819
626317LV00001B/193/P